WOL

Cumbria

SPYNOSAUR
THE SPY'S THE LIMIT!

I'm *under* cover!

SPYN

DEPARTMENT 6 ●○○✕≡

CLASSIFILE #07-09-MMXVII

STRIPES PUBLISHING, an imprint of the Little Tiger Group
1 Coda Studios, 189 Munster Road, London SW6 6AW
A paperback original
First published in Great Britain in 2017

Text copyright © Guy Bass, 2017
Illustrations copyright © Lee Robinson, 2017

ISBN: 978-1-84715-814-7

A CIP catalogue record for this book is available
from the British Library.

Printed and bound in the UK.
10 9 8 7 6 5 4 3 2 1

DEPARTMENT
6

OSAUR

IN THE SPY'S THE LIMIT!

GUY BASS ILLUSTRATED BY LEE ROBINSON

To Joe and Arianne
Thanks for the gadgets!
– Guy Bass

For Dad
Hopefully this book sells
loads of copies and I can pay
you that money back.
– Lee Robinson

Stripes

When top *spy*-entists put the mind of super-spy Agent Gambit inside the body of a dinosaur, they created the first ever **Super Secret Agent Dinosaur**. Together with his daughter, Amber, this prehistoric hero protects the world from villainy.

His code name:

SPYNOSAUR

FROM A LAND BEFORE TIME COMES A HERO FOR TODAY...

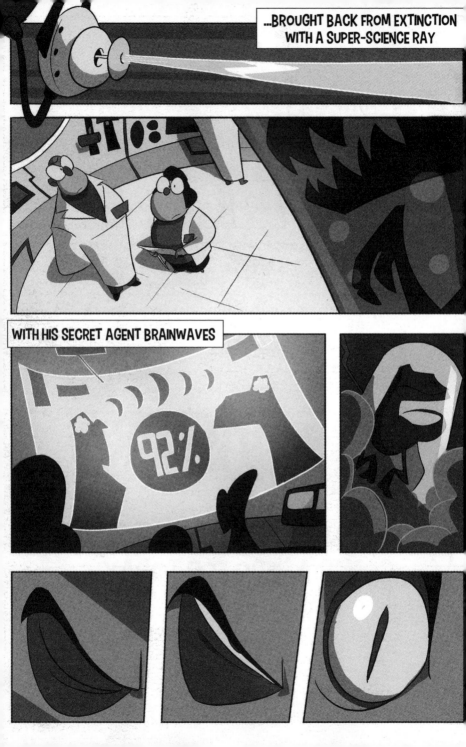

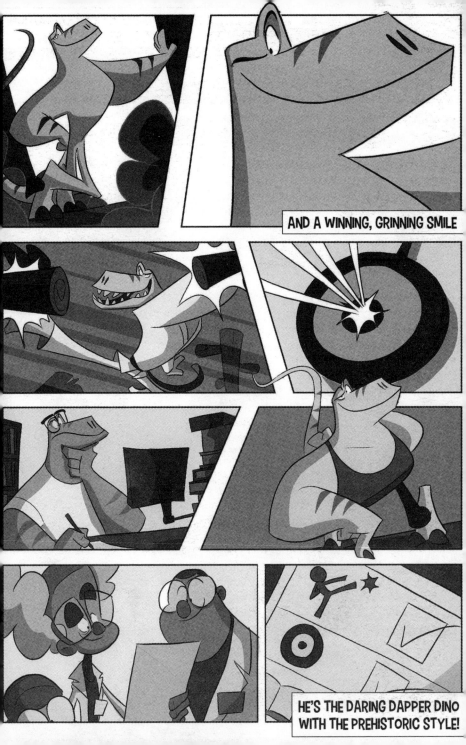

AND A WINNING, GRINNING SMILE

HE'S THE DARING DAPPER DINO WITH THE PREHISTORIC STYLE!

HE'S THE SCALED 'N' TAILED AGENT WHO IS CERTAIN TO SURPRISE

BUT HE STILL LOOKS LIKE A DINOSAUR, WHATEVER HIS DISGUISE

SPYNOSAUR!

1.
HOW AMBER SPENT HER WEEKEND

"Amber Gambit!"

Amber sat up with a start. Her teacher was glowering at her.

"I'm sure your daydreams can't possibly be as exciting as your writing assignment ... can they?"

Amber was pretty sure this was a trick question.

"Uh, no, Miss," she replied. She looked down at her exercise book. In it she'd written the words:

HOW I SPENT MY WEEKEND
by Amber Gambit

Amber chewed the end of her pencil and cast her mind back over the past forty-eight hours.

HOW AMBER ACTUALLY SPENT HER WEEKEND

Her pencil hovered over the paper.

"Hmm, better not," she sighed. Then she wrote:

I went to the cinema.

Amber looked down at her Super Secret Spy Watch™. She longed to hear its *BA-DEEP BA-DEEP BA-DEEP*, signalling the start of another mission ... but the watch remained silent. Amber leaned back in her chair and stared up at the ceiling.

A short, old man with a craggy face stared back at her.

"AA— mff!" cried Amber, slapping her hand over her mouth mid-scream. She checked to make sure no one else had noticed the man dangling from the ceiling on a wire. He was Amber's height, wore a school uniform identical to hers and sported a red wig very much like Amber's own hair.

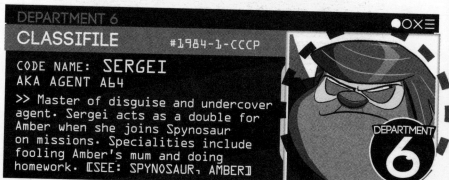

DEPARTMENT 6

●○✕☰

CLASSIFILE   #1984-1-CCCP

CODE NAME: SERGEI
AKA AGENT A64
>> Master of disguise and undercover agent. Sergei acts as a double for Amber when she joins Spynosaur on missions. Specialities include fooling Amber's mum and doing homework. [SEE: SPYNOSAUR, AMBER]

DEPARTMENT 6

"Sergei!" she hissed. "What are you doing here?"

"Sergei is doing Sergei's job," he replied. "When Amber goes on mission, Sergei replaces Amber and no one knows difference. Except for improvement in schoolwork."

"Wait, there's a mission?" Amber whispered.

"No, Sergei is here because school dinners are so delicious," Sergei replied. "Sergei is being sarcastic. In school canteen they do not even serve pickled hoof of goat or smoked fish heads. How do they expect children to grow up strong like bear?"

"Uh, Sergei ... the mission?" Amber prompted him.

"Oh, yes – Spynosaur is waiting for you," Sergei said. "Get to toilet, quick!"

2.
DOUBLE FLUSH

With Sergei in place at her desk, Amber used her ninja skills to crawl, silent and unseen, under her classmates' tables and out of the classroom. She raced to the girls' toilet, hurried into the third cubicle and sat down.

"Voice *Spy-dentification:* Amber Gambit," she whispered into her Super Secret Spy Watch™. "Double Flush."

A tinny, automated voice replied:

VOICE SPY-DENTIFICATION CONFIRMED. HAVE A SAFE FLIGHT, AMBER.

The ceiling and roof slid aside above Amber's head to reveal a blue sky. Amber grinned and flushed the toilet twice.

"Up, up and—"

FWOOOOOOOOSH!

"AWAAhahahahahaha!" cried Amber as the toilet blasted, rocket-like, into the air!

Amber held on tight as the loo streaked skywards, up and up, through the clouds and beyond. Then, as the toilet's boosters finally began to sputter, she heard the familiar hum of her dad's almost-invisible jet-plane, the Dino-soarer. She saw a hazy shimmer in the sky, and a moment later she and the toilet were swallowed inside the Dino-soarer's docking bay.

DEPARTMENT 6 ●○⊗☰

CLASSIFILE #1984-DZ-DB8

CODE NAME:
THE DINO-SOARER
>> Supersonic saurian-styled stealth jet. Specially adapted for pilots with tails. Equipped with invisibility mode, gravity beam, missile launchers, front and rear laser cannons and built-in Wi-Fi.

DEPARTMENT 6

"Rocket Toilet is my new favourite thing!" said Amber, hopping off the loo. She slipped into her spy-suit and made her way through the Dino-soarer, past a pair of jet packs and a folding car to the cockpit, to find her dad in the pilot's seat.

"Ready to save the world again, Amber?" he asked.

Amber's dad, it's safe to say, wasn't like other dads. Not because he was the world's greatest secret agent or because he saved the world at least twice a month. Amber's dad was different because he was a *dinosaur*.

"Didn't we save the world just yesterday?" Amber chuckled, leaping into the co-pilot's seat.

The world's most daring (and only) secret agent dinosaur flashed a grin filled with sharp teeth.

"We did indeed. Fortunately I'm always ready to be uncommonly remarkable at a moment's notice," replied Spynosaur, a glint in his lizard eye. "Department 6 picked up a coded distress signal coming through its top-secret transmission channel. It's an old code but it checks out – and it's coming from somewhere in the Arctic Circle. Could be a little nippy..."

"I don't care where we're going!" Amber replied giddily. "Being a super secret agent—"

"Super secret agent *in training*," corrected her dad.

"...Is easily a million and twelve times better than school," continued Amber. "Spying's better than crisps or comics or rocket toilets or—"

FORTY-SIX MINUTES LATER...

"I've changed my m-mind!" Amber screamed. "I w-want to go b-back to school!"

A freezing, howling blizzard battered her as she followed Spynsoaur through the Arctic snow. The Dino-soarer's gravity ray had deposited them in the middle of a storm so fierce that Amber could barely see her hand in front of her face. And, despite her anti-outside-world thermalizing onesie, she had never been so cold.

"Stay close — you can bathe in the warmth of my impressiveness," said her dad, pulling his fur-collared arctic jacket closer. He checked the coordinates on his Super Secret Spy Watch™. "We're close to the source of the signal. Keep your *ice* peeled, Amber..."

"Da-ad, no p-puns!" Amber howled. "Even the *p-p-penguins* groaned at that one..."

"Penguins?" Spynosaur repeated, peering through the blizzard. Sure enough, a pair of penguins were waddling awkwardly towards them, their heads cocked curiously to one side. "Well spotted, Amber – you're *spy-sight* is getting better every day," he added. "There's only one problem..."

"What's that?" Amber asked.

"There *are* no penguins in the Arctic," Spynosaur replied. His eyes narrowed as he peered closer. "If my super-spy senses are right – and they're never wrong – these are *man-made musical mecha-penguins*! Cover your ears!"

9.
MENACE OF THE MAN-MADE MUSICAL MECHA-PENGUINS

Without warning, the penguins' heads ratcheted open at the mouth, flipping backwards with a robotic **VRRRR** to reveal a mass of mechanics.

"As I suspected! Cybernetic subwoofer speaker systems!" cried Spynosaur before the nearest penguin let out an ear-splitting B flat.

AAEEEEEEEIIIEE!

Spynsoaur and Amber clamped their hands over their ears as the other penguin joined in with a deafening yet perfectly pitched note. Within seconds, the bionic birds' stunning sounds had brought the spies to their knees.

EEEEOOEEEE!

Spynosaur had just enough strength to draw his pistol from his shoulder holster, but the penguins' cruel chorus was so dizzying he couldn't focus enough to aim. Out of the corner of his eye he saw an overcome Amber slump, unconscious, into the snow.

OOEEAAEEEEEEE EEEEEEEEEEEE!

As the birds' ballad grew even more brutal, Spynosaur felt his consciousness start to slip away ... then he felt a sudden rumble as the snow began to shake and shift. The ice cracked again and again, splintering beneath him. With his last ounce of strength, Spynosaur scooped Amber up in his arms and leaped into the air as a great dome of ice suddenly blasted out of the ground, sending both penguins flying. The tuneful terrors landed in the snow on their backs, and found themselves unable to get up. They immediately fell silent but for the odd robotic wheeze, rocking and flapping helplessly.

"D-Dad?" Amber grunted as she came round. She sat up and rubbed her temples. "The p-p-penguins, what h-happened...?"

"A design flaw – it seems these *ro-birds* cannot sing on their backs," Spynosaur explained as the penguins struggled soundlessly. "Of course, I would've worked that out just in the nick of time but I suspect whoever made that giant igloo grow out of the ice knew it already."

As Spynosaur helped Amber to her feet, she peered through the blizzard at the igloo, a frozen hemisphere built from enormous slabs of ice.

"What n-now?" asked a shivering Amber.

"I'd say we've just been sent an invitation," replied Spynsoaur, brushing the snow off his pistol. "Let's say hello, shall we?"

Spynosaur and Amber trudged through the snow to the igloo's entrance and peered in. A dark tunnel led inside the dome.

"Stay close," whispered Spynosaur as they made their way down the tunnel towards a dim, flickering light. "My uncanny spy senses tell me we can expect trouble with a capital T, and quite possibly R-O-U-B-L-E."

Spynosaur and Amber emerged in the innards of the igloo. What they found could not have been further from the hostility of the snowstorm. The large room was lit only by a roaring log fire at the far end. Wood panelling covered the walls and a crystal chandelier hung from the ceiling. Ornate furniture filled the space – tables, chests, sofas, even a grand piano.

"If this is a rescue mission, you're thirty years too late," said a clipped voice. "But then you always did like to dilly-dally, *boy*."

Spynosaur and Amber looked round. A figure was sitting in a high-backed armchair by the fire.

"'Boy'?" repeated Spynosaur, turning the most

peculiar shade of pale green.

The figure rose from the chair. The light from the fire danced across his face, revealing a lean, bespectacled man with greying hair. He was dressed in a crisp, brown tweed suit.

Spynosaur took a step back. "Impossible," he muttered at last. "*Dad?*"

4.
ABNER GAMBIT (AKA AGENT A1, AKA SPYNOSAUR'S DAD)

"Put that away, boy – problems are not solved with *guns*," said the man.

"Sorry, Dad," Spynosaur said, hastily holstering his pistol.

"Wait. 'DAD'? As in, Granddad?" Amber blurted.

The man picked up a nearby cane and strode across the room towards them.

"You – you're alive," Spynosaur gasped. "But you're dead!"

"Well, which is it? I clearly cannot be both," Spynosaur's father tutted. "Any spy worth their salt should have no problem deducing why I am standing here, alive and well in a drawing-room igloo in the North Pole, having barely aged a day in –" the man took a moment to check his watch – "over thirty years." He glared at Spynosaur. "So, you're a dinosaur now, are you, boy? How predictably *flash*."

"Yes, I am an impressive sight to— Wait, how did you even know it was me?" said Spynosaur. "The last time I saw you—"

"You were a ten-year-old agent in training," interrupted Spynosaur's dad. He jabbed his cane in Spynosaur's direction. "And, to answer your question, I know of no one else who would be happy to parade around like *that*. I mean, look at you! The claws, the teeth, the tail ... you always did enjoy showing off but this is ridiculous. Spying is about blending in, not standing out."

"It's not my fault. I was tied to a space rocket

and fired into the moon," Spynosaur replied defensively. "Then the Department 6 *spy-entists* put my brainwaves into the body of a—"

Spynosaur's dad held up his hand dismissively.

"I'll read the report," he said, before turning to Amber. "Now, who is this?"

Amber immediately stood up straight. (Her granddad seemed to be a man who liked people to stand up straight.)

"Uh, this is Amber … my daughter," Spynosaur replied. "Amber, this is your grandfather, Abner Gambit."

"I have a granddaughter?" Abner Gambit laughed in delight. "Bless my suicide tooth! My dear Amber, what a singular pleasure to meet you!"

Amber wasn't ready for an embrace from a grandfather she'd never met in an igloo at the North Pole … but the hug turned out to be warm and comfy, with a faint whiff of gunpowder and shoe polish.

"And look, you're a secret agent!" he added, inspecting her with unbridled admiration.

"Secret agent *in training*," Spynosaur corrected.

"Pish-posh, she's a born spy. You can tell just from looking at her!" Abner declared.

"Want to see some ninja moves?" Amber asked.

"Nothing would give me more pleasure!" replied Abner. Amber immediately started chopping and kicking the air.

"UNSEEN BONY ELBOW PENCIL CASE SHADOW ATTACK!"

"Remarkable! " Abner chuckled. "You mark my words, boy, this girl will be out-spying you in no time ... if she isn't already."

"You – you really think so?" Amber asked.

"Indubitably!" Abner replied. "Why, I'll wager you're the second greatest secret agent in the world ... after your old granddad."

"But what happened to you?" Spynosaur said, rubbing his temples with clawed fingers. "Your last mission – you were pursuing the Purple Spyder..."

"Who's the Purple Spyder?" Amber asked.

"Excellent question, Amber. Truly, you have the curious mind of a spy!" Abner said, making Amber's cheeks flush red. "The Purple Spyder is as deadly as poison and as silent as drying paint. He is the *Other Side*'s number one agent, and the most frustrating pain in the—"

"There is no 'Other Side', Dad, not any more," explained Spynosaur. "The days of rival spy agencies are a thing of the past. Today agents from all over the world work *together* to defeat the evil plots of flamboyantly diabolical would-be world-conquering villains like—"

"You concern yourself with criminals and their

cartoonish plots if you wish, boy," Abner tutted. "I choose to focus on the real danger — spies!"

"We're getting off the point," Spynosaur snarled in frustration. "I searched for you forever, Dad! What happened to you? What are you doing here? Where have you been for thirty years?"

"I would have thought that was obvious to anyone with a modicum of wit," Abner replied. He took out a piece of paper from his pocket and unfolded it. From his other pocket he produced a fountain pen and began to doodle. "But since your powers of deduction appear to have abandoned you, allow me to draw you a picture..."

"Da-ad, there's no need to—" Spynosaur began but it was too late. Abner held up the piece of paper and waved it in front of his son's face.

ME ON A MISSION

MUST STOP PURPLE SPYDER

ME CHASING SPYDER. CHASE! CHASE!

THE SPYDER'S SECRET BASE AT THE NORTH POLE

SURRENDER, PLEASE

OH NO! HIDDEN WEAPON! (FREEZE BOMB)

WHACK!

FREEZE!

...

"So you chased a baddie spy to the North Pole and he froze you both in ice?" Amber gasped.

"See? Your ten-year-old daughter understands perfectly, boy – I don't see why you're so confused," said Abner. "Regardless, frozen I remained until yesterday, at around teatime," he added. "I awoke to find the room – and myself – quite thawed out. I quickly improvised a top-secret signal-transmitter using an old telephone, a box of matches and my least favourite cufflinks. And here – eventually – you are."

"We must be a sight for *thaw* eyes," said Spynosaur.

"Da-ad, no puns," Amber groaned. "Unless ... do *you* like puns, Granddad?"

"Absolutely not. Puns are for the playground – spying is serious business," Abner replied. "Speaking of which, I have a mission to complete. I'm sure it hasn't escaped your attention that the

Purple Spyder is nowhere to be seen. Clearly he defrosted rather sooner than I did and beat a hasty retreat. His sky-car is gone and, from the footprints he left in the bearskin rug, I'd say he has a full day's head start. We must act fast."

"Dad, you've been in a block of ice for thirty years," Spynosaur began. "I'm not sure you're in any fit state to—"

"Are you not listening, boy?" Abner said sternly. "The Purple Spyder is on the loose! He must be stopped or, I promise you, Department 6 – and the very future of spying – is doomed!"

"Sounds like a mission to me," said Amber excitedly.

"It does indeed, *Agent* Amber," replied her granddad, clacking his cane loudly on the floor. "And there's no time to waste – lead the way!"

5.
THE SPY WHO CAME IN FROM THE EXTREME COLD

DEPARTMENT 6 HEADQUARTERS, BENEATH THE NATURAL HISTORY MUSEUM OF LONDON, LONDON

The Dino-soarer conveyed Spynosaur, Amber and Abner to London at supersonic speeds. Amber was pretty sure she could have cut the tension between her dad and granddad with the hidden laser in her Super Secret Spy Watch™. They didn't seem to agree on anything.

"No doubt your father told you spying is all

about blowing things to smithereens," Abner suggested, running his finger along the Dino-soarer's dashboard to check for dust.

"Well, uh..." Amber began, not sure how to respond.

"It's worked pretty well for us so far, hasn't it, Amber?" Spynosaur said with a wink. "At least I don't just *talk* my enemies to death..."

"True spying is about *spy-chology*, Amber — understanding how the enemy thinks," Abner retorted. "In all my years as a secret agent, I have never once donned a silly disguise or used a gadget or had to blow anything up at all."

"I think Amber prefers the non-stop adrenaline-fuelled thrill-ride of *modern* spying," Spynosaur replied.

"And she is clever enough to know that a blunt instrument is no substitute for a sharp mind," Abner retorted, tapping the side of his head with his cane.

And so the bickering went on. Amber couldn't have been more relieved when the Dino-soarer finally landed on the roof of the Natural History Museum. The three spies were deposited down a chimney and sped through metallic transport tubes before emerging with a **FWOOOMP** into Department 6's underground headquarters. But before their feet had even touched the ground...

"Spynosaur!"

Spynosaur and Amber turned to see the head of Department 6, M11, striding towards them, her moustache twitching angrily.

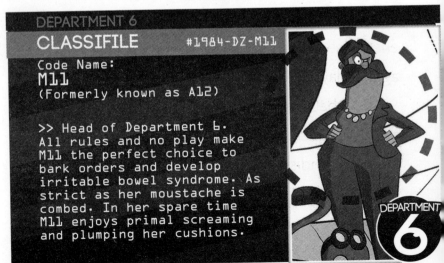

DEPARTMENT 6

CLASSIFILE   #1984-DZ-M11

Code Name:
M11
(Formerly known as A12)

>> Head of Department 6.
All rules and no play make
M11 the perfect choice to
bark orders and develop
irritable bowel syndrome. As
strict as her moustache is
combed. In her spare time
M11 enjoys primal screaming
and plumping her cushions.

DEPARTMENT
6

"Spynosaur, you maddening maverick! You're the reason my therapist is a rich man!" she continued. "Does it ever occur to you to report in? Or are you too busy showing off for a simple call? We've been on tenterhooks waiting to hear from ... from..."

M11's jaw dropped as she set eyes upon a man she thought was lost forever.

"Ab-Abner?" she stuttered. "Abner Gambit?"

"Agent A12, as I live and breathe," Abner said with a smile, peering at M11 over his spectacles. "Although I see you're wearing the Moustache of Seniority now. I knew you'd end up running this place."

"Yes, it's – it's M11 now." M11 stroked her moustache awkwardly – and for the first time ever, Amber saw her blush. "But you – you haven't aged a day!" M11 added. "How...?"

"Ah, that..." Abner said. "My apologies for not being in touch in the last thirty years. I'm afraid I was quite indisposed."

"You could say he was left out in the *cold*," Spynosaur began. "You see, Dad had a rather *frosty* reception from—"

"Da-ad..." Amber huffed.

"Yes, do hush, boy," Abner tutted.

"I – we – didn't think I'd – we'd – ever see you again," said a flustered M11. "But here you are ... Abner Gambit, the man who wrote the rule book on spying."

She reached into a pocket and took out a small, leather-bound book as a crowd of agents gathered round, eager to catch sight of long-lost Agent A1.

"Wait, you wrote the *actual* rule book?" Amber gasped.

"I assume your father never bothered to show you it," Abner said. "He never did like rules … he's got too much of his mother in him."

"Mother….?" Spynosaur whispered. Amber had never heard her dad mention his mother before. Spynosaur reached into a pocket and took out a silver locket. He opened it and stared wistfully for a long three seconds.

"You OK, Dad?" Amber asked.

Spynosaur hastily slipped the locket back into his spy-suit. "Couldn't be better," he said quickly.

"Perhaps talent skips a generation," suggested Abner loudly. "Because from what I've seen, Agent Amber here has what it takes to be a spy without equal. I suggest you keep an eye on her, M11 — she'll be after your job in no time!"

Then it was Amber's turn to blush.

6.
THE WORLD'S GREATEST SECRET AGENT

"So it's true!" came a sudden cry. An impractically tall man with an explosion of hair and wearing a white coat pushed past the other agents and began shaking Abner's hand.

DEPARTMENT 6

CLASSIFILE   #1687-AAPL

●○○✕≡

CODE NAME:
DR NEWTOWN NEWFANGLE, PHD, BTW, ROTFL

>> Department 6's top spy-entist, gadget guru, frustrated rapper. Creator of the Variable Science Ray Beam Emitter ⟦SEE: RONALD RAY-GUN⟧, used to grow the dinosaur body that houses the mind of Agent Gambit ⟦SEE: SPYNOSAUR⟧

DEPARTMENT
6

"Ah, Dr Newfangle," Spynosaur said. "I don't think you ever met my—"

"Agent A1!" shrieked Dr Newfangle. "A1 ... Abner Gambit ... the world's greatest secret agent!"

"I thought I was the world's greatest— Never mind," Spynosaur sighed.

"Out of the way!" howled another voice. "Move, or I'll untie yer laces! I'll scuff yer shoe polish! I'll pull down one of yer socks an' leave yer legs lookin' lopsided!"

A spider-monkey dressed in a spy-suit skidded to a halt in front of Abner Gambit.

DEPARTMENT 6

CLASSIFILE   #2-MALPA

CODE NAME: DANGER MONKEY
AKA AGENT A41

>> The second secret agent to have his mind transferred into a spy-entifically modified body after Spynosaur. [SEE: SPYNOSAUR, DR NEWFANGLE] Attempts to make a second dinosaur body failed, so Dr Newfangle made him a monkey. Doesn't like people making a monkey of him.

DEPARTMENT
6

"Danger Monkey!" began Spynosaur. "I'd like to introduce—"

"Abner Gambit, as I live an' breathe!" shrieked Danger Monkey, hugging Abner round the left leg like a long-lost love. "I never dreamed I'd get t' meet you in the flesh, but 'ere I am, suckin' in the same air as the World's Greatest Secret Agent!"

By now, Amber's jaw was almost on the floor. Everyone thought her granddad was the best spy ever! Even better than – she hardly dared to think it – even better than her dad.

"Well, things have certainly ... moved on in the last thirty years," Abner said, trying to shake Danger Monkey from his leg. "But I don't want any fuss – a true spy cares not for glory or—"

"Too late!" cried Danger Monkey and Dr Newfangle together. Then they whipped hidden microphones from secret pockets ... and Abner Gambit's rap began.

7.
THE P.L.O.T.
DEVICE

"Your enthusiastic tributes, though confusing, are much appreciated," noted Abner Gambit as Dr Newfangle and Danger Monkey dropped their microphones dramatically. "It's good to know that the Department still appreciates a *real* spy in this day and—"

"Excuse me, Dad," Spynosaur interrupted, "but I thought you had a mission to complete. Why don't you tell everyone what you told us back in the Dino-soarer?"

"Thank you for reminding me how to do a job I

was doing while you were still soiling your nappy, boy," Abner replied. He made his way to a nearby computer and sat down in front of it. "How very shiny," he added as he tapped the keyboard. "But let us see if it holds an old secret or two..."

PASSWORD ACCEPTED.

TOP SECRET ACCESS GRANTED.

Abner paused, and typed again.

PASSED PASSWORD ACCEPTED.

TOPPEST TOP SECRET ACCESS GRANTED.

"*Toppest* Top Secret?" M11 barked. "Blast it to smithereens, what in the name of grammatical horrors is 'Toppest Top' Secret?"

"You know how it is with secrets and spies," replied Abner, raising an eyebrow. "Ladies and gentlemen, yesterday – or rather, thirty years ago – an enemy agent known as the Purple Spyder broke into these very headquarters, here at Department 6."

"The Purple Spyder? I thought he was a myth!" declared M11. "I mean, I heard rumours of his existence back in spy school but I assumed he was a fable to scare young spies-in-training..."

"I can assure you, the Spyder is quite real – and he stole something of vital importance from us," Abner continued. He pressed a final key and an image of a small, gloss-black cube appeared on screen. "Behold, the *Predictive Lexicon Oracle Tracer* – otherwise known as the P.L.O.T. Device."

"The P.L.O.T. Device? I thought it was a myth!" Dr Newfangle declared, staring at the cube. "I mean, I heard rumours of its existence back in spy-ence school, but—"

"Also real," Abner interrupted. "You see, villains and their plots are easily foiled, but there is nothing more dangerous than a spy who is *not on your side*. So, using complex artificial intelligence, advanced algorithms and pointless astrology, Department 6 spy-entists created a device capable of deducing the identities of every spy on Earth."

"Deducing? Identities? Every?" M11 gasped. "But our work, our lives, our identities are top secret! Not even my pet Labrador, Isambard Kingdom Brunel, knows that I'm a spy!"

"I'm afraid no agent is safe from the P.L.O.T. Device. Not you, M11 ... not this costumed monkey ... not even..."

"Not even..." repeated Spynosaur, waiting for his dad to say his name.

"Not even my granddaughter," added Abner. "She may only be a secret agent in training but the P.L.O.T. Device knows Amber Gambit is a *born* spy!"

Amber blushed again, not caring half as much as she should have done that her secret life as a spy could be on the verge of being exposed.

"When the Purple Spyder deciphers the information on the P.L.O.T. Device, he will reveal all of our secret identities to the world," Abner concluded. "Department 6 will be *doomed.*"

"That dirty device!" Danger Monkey howled. "I'll smash its circuits! I'll mash its mainframe! I'll drop it down the toilet and cause irreparable water damage!"

"Well, we can't have your mother finding out what you get up to, eh, Amber?" Spynosaur said.

Amber nodded. There was no way her mum would agree to her going on death-defyingly dangerous missions at least twice a week.

"Blast it to smithereens! The Purple Spyder must be stopped!" M11 howled. "But how do we find him? How do we know where he's—?"

"Tokyo, Japan," Abner interrupted. "That's where the Purple Spyder is headed."

"How d'you fathom that?" asked Danger Monkey, picking a flea out of his fur and eating it.

"It's very simple," said Spynosaur, before his dad could reply. "The Purple Spyder is unnaturally fond of the colour purple. The word 'purple' is an anagram of 'ruppel'. Mr Ruppel was my grade two piano teacher. Pianos have eighty-eight keys. Keys open doors, as do handles. George Frederick Handel was a composer, who had a little-known allergy to cheese. Cheese rhymes with please. Please and thank you. Thank you for the music. Music to my ears. *Ear* today, gone tomorrow. Tomorrow is another day. It's been six hundred and sixty *days* since Danger Monkey last took a shower. And six hundred and sixty *thousand* is the tonnage of fish sold annually at the Tokyo Fish Market – an ideal hideout for a spy with something fishy on his mind."

"Blimey!" cried Danger Monkey.

"And – if my son has quite finished showing off – I stole the Spyder's address book when last we fought," said Abner, taking a purple notebook from his pocket. "He wrote the location of his Tokyo hideout right here."

"Blast it to smithereens, there's no time to waste!" barked M11. "Spynosaur, you and your sidekick accompany Agent A1 to Tokyo. Your mission: retrieve the P.L.O.T. Device," M11 commanded, her moustache twitching impatiently. "And blast it to smithereens, Spynosaur – try not to blow anything to smithereens!"

8.
SOMETHING FISHY

TOKYO FISH MARKET, TOKYO, JAPAN

"We're closing in on the Purple Spyder's hideout," explained Abner as he, Spynosaur and Amber made their way through the bustling streets of Japan's capital city. "I suggest we keep a low profile until we can flush him out."

"Low profile, got it," said Spynosaur. He was wearing a traditional Japanese *kimono* embroidered with pictures of flowers, an elaborate black wig and tall wooden sandals, which CLIP-ed and CLOP-ed loudly as he walked down the street, his tail swishing behind him. His face was painted white, with a precise dot of bright red lipstick over his lips.

"A true spy blends into his surroundings without the need for disguises, boy," Abner huffed. "And while you may have fooled these simple folk, the Spyder will see through you in an instant. I understand our enemy's *spy-chology* ... I know how he thinks. The Spyder is cunning and devious; he keeps friends in high and low places; he can turn any object into a weapon and sets deadly *traps* for anyone who crosses him. Where the Purple Spyder goes, danger follows."

"Sounds like you're not a *fan*," said Spynosaur, opening a bamboo hand fan with an elaborate flourish as they rounded a corner into the fish market. "Don't worry, we've been waiting for an enemy we can get our *claws* into, eh, Amber?"

Amber didn't reply — and not just because her dad's puns were terrible. The sight of the market had stopped her in her tracks. She'd never seen so many people crammed together in one place. The long street was so dense with shoppers it was like a human river flowing into the far distance. On both sides of the street were countless stalls, selling seafood of every description.

"So ... many ... fish," muttered Amber in awe.

"Exactly – so a Spyder should stand out like a sore, purple thumb," said Spynosaur, giving Amber a wink. "First one to find him gets to snag him in Dr Newfangle's new spy-net!"

With that, Amber dived into the crowd, shuffling past shoppers or darting between their legs.

"Must you treat everything like a game, boy?" tutted Abner, polishing the top of his cane.

"Look, Dad, I know we didn't always see eye to eye," Spynosaur said, "and I know I wasn't always the best pupil when it came to spy training..."

"Why don't we save reminiscing until *after* the mission is complete," Abner replied.

Spynosaur shook his head and sighed a long sigh. Then: "Dad!"

At the sound of his daughter's panicked cry, Spynosaur immediately leaped into action.

"Wait, boy!" Abner cried. "It's surely a trap!"

"Isn't it always!" cried Spynosaur, knocking shoppers for six as he raced through the crowds.

"Daaad!" Amber cried again.

Spynosaur scanned the thronged street with his uncanny spy-sight. Then, after a long second, he saw it.

A flash of purple.

A motionless figure stood still and silent in the river of people. He was tall and lean, with a bright purple trench coat, suit and hat. A purple mask emblazoned with the silhouette of a spider covered his entire face. And tucked under his right arm, held in a vice-like grip, was Amber.

"Lemme go, you purple stinker!" Amber cried, struggling in vain to break free. "Also, give us the P.L.O.T. Device!"

Spynosaur tore off his disguise. At the sight of a real, live dinosaur, the crowd panicked, scattering like frightened fish as Spynosaur pushed onwards. Within moments he was eye to eye with his new enemy.

"The Purple Spyder, I presume," said Spynosaur. "You know, you *cod* have chosen a less crowded *plaice* for a face-off."

Amber just had enough time to say "Da-ad" before the Spyder skewered the collar of her spy-suit on to a wall-mounted fish hook, leaving her dangling. As Amber howled in protest, the Spyder remained as silent as a photograph, no hint of emotion visible beneath his spider-emblazoned mask. "I've been *herring* rumours that you can use any object as a weapon," Spynosaur continued, "but I'm afraid you're out of luck, since there's nothing here except—"

SLAP!

A fish hit Spynosaur hard in the face! The Spyder was so swift, Spynosaur didn't even see him fling it.

"Ow," he said, rubbing his chin. "Now hang on a—"

SLUP!
SLAP!

In a blur of movement, the Spyder had hurled two more fish through the air. They hit Spynosaur square in the eyes.

"You're *skate*-ing on *fin* ice, Spyder!" Spynosaur said, wiping fish scales from his face. The Spyder plucked two squid from a nearby crate and swung them round like fighting sticks. Spynosaur reached for his pistol, and then a much more reckless idea occurred to him. He picked up two fat fish and spun them in his hands. "An old-fashioned fish fight, eh? That suits me just *brine*."

9. FISH FIGHT!

A FISH RIGHT IN THE FACE WON'T STOP OUR HERO SPYNOSAUR

HE'LL KEEP ON KEEPING ON AND KEEP ON COMING BACK FOR MORE!

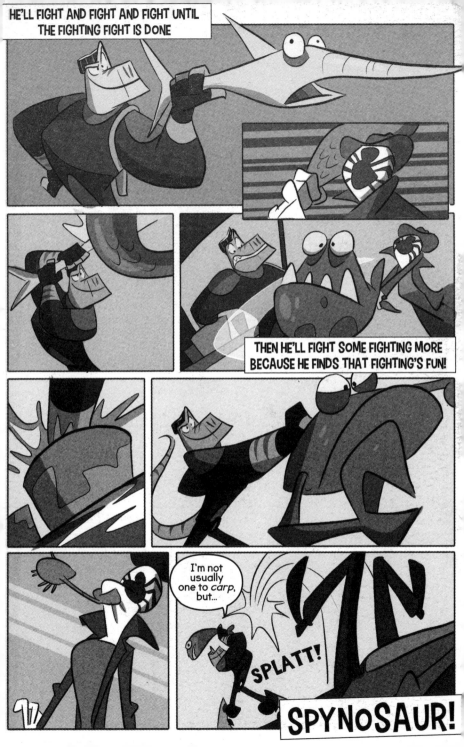

The Spyder crashed into a stall, crumpling into a purple heap among a mound of mackerel.

"I'd say that knocked him off his *perch*," said Spynosaur. "Activate spy-net!" He pressed a button on his left wrist and with a **FOOOOSH** a wide net made of super-fine steel mesh launched out from a secret compartment on his sleeve, enveloping the Spyder where he lay.

"He's a tough one, and no mist-*hake*," began Spynosaur, unhooking Amber from the wall and placing her on the ground. "But I don't think he understands the *scale* of my—"

"Da-ad, look!" Amber cried.

Spynosaur spun round to see the Purple Spyder, already free of the spy-net and racing down a narrow alleyway. Spynosaur and his sidekick gave chase, pursuing the Spyder through the alleyway and into a wide warehouse, packed with crate after crate of fish. The Spyder was dizzyingly fast

— he was already halfway across the warehouse and speeding towards the exit.

"The purple stinker's getting away!" Amber howled.

"Actually he's surrounded," said a voice as cool as a fridge full of cucumbers. From behind a stack of crates emerged Abner Gambit, blocking the Spyder's escape route. The Spyder skidded to a halt in the centre of the warehouse as Spynosaur and Amber closed in behind him. "Spying is not about the chase, it's about knowing where the chase ends," Abner added. "There is nowhere to run, Spyder. Now tell us where you have hidden the P.L.O.T. Device!"

The Purple Spyder cocked his masked head to one side ... then raised both arms high, as if to surrender.

"Good choice," said Spynosaur, taking a pair of hi-tech handcuffs from his belt. "I've *haddock* enough of chasing you anyway..."

"Wait, boy!" said Abner. "The Spyder would never surrender without first setting a ... trap..."

Abner fell silent as the Purple Spyder reached down and took off his hat. Upon the Spyder's head sat a small, black cube.

"The P.L.O.T. Device!" Abner cried. "Give me that!"

Abner leaped at the Spyder, failing to spot the near-invisible grappling claw, which launched silently upwards out of the Spyder's sleeve.

"He's got a ghost claw!" Spynosaur cried, diving towards the Spyder from behind. "Dad, stop!"

As the grappling claw skewered the ceiling, a section of the floor fell away like a trap door. The Spyder retracted the ghost claw and swiftly ascended, crashing through the ceiling to freedom ... while Abner and Spynosaur found themselves plummeting into a pool of freezing water.

"Dad! Granddad!" Amber cried as Spynosaur and Abner were flung out of the water and crashed on to the warehouse floor.

"We're – *koff!* – we're all right," gasped Spynosaur, helping Abner to his feet. "But I wouldn't like to make a *halibut* of it."

"Is everything a joke to you, boy?" Abner hissed. "If you hadn't let the Spyder slip through your clumsy claws, we would have the P.L.O.T. Device!"

"Now hang on," replied Spynosaur. "I like wrestling a giant octopus as much as the next spy but I'm no *sucker*. If you hadn't rushed the Spyder, then—"

"I, boy? *I* was the world's greatest secret agent before you were potty-trained," Abner retorted. "Did I not teach you everything you know about spying?"

"Yes, but—" Spynosaur began.

"Then I'd prefer if you didn't tell me how to do my job," Abner continued. He wafted his cane in Spynosaur's direction. "After all, if you'd paid more attention to my training, you might not have ended up as ... *that*."

In that moment, Amber decided she would rather face an *army* of giant octopuses than listen to grown-ups argue. And, since her dad and granddad were both brilliant spies, their arguing didn't even make sense. Amber did her best to break the tension.

"Uh, any other addresses in the purple stinker's book, Granddad?" she asked.

"Excellent idea!" Abner said, tuning his back on Spynosaur as he took the Spyder's notebook out of his pocket. "Your mind is as keen and honed as your ninja skills, Agent Amber."

That was more than enough to lift Amber's spirits. She cried, "**UNDEFEATABLE OMELETTE RACEHORSE SUPERGLUE KICK!**" and spun in the air, kicking her legs wildly.

"If I know the Spyder's spy-chology, which I do, he will be looking for protection now he knows we're on to him," Abner surmised, thumbing through the notebook. But where will he— Aha! Here's something..."

"Let me guess," said Spynosaur. "*Bronzeface*."

Abner glanced up over his spectacles. "You peeked," he sneered.

"Not at all ... it's very simple," Spynosaur explained. "The Purple Spyder wears a hat. 'Hat' rhymes with 'cat' and 'rat' but not 'guinea pig'. Guinea pigs are the sixth most popular pet. Six is the number of legs on an ant, except for the Lithuanian Limping Ant, which has only five. Five, four, three, two, one. One in a million. And one million *dollars* is the current bounty on the head of Da Big City's Big Boss of Big Bosses – the go-to gangster for high-class, high-cost protection, Donnie Bronzeface."

Amber glanced at the address book. Upon the open page was written:

Donnie D Bronzeface
No.1305 Undaworld St
Da Big City
USA
bestprotectioneveryonesaysso@Bronzeface.com

"Da Big City! I've always wanted to go there," Amber squealed.

"If we can get to the Spyder before he reaches Bronzeface, we might even secure the P.L.O.T. Device without any more drama," Abner remarked.

"Let's hope not," said Spynosaur. "But I can get us there in record time. Come on!"

Abner and Amber followed Spynosaur back out on to the street, now deserted but for fish. Spynosaur tapped his Super Secret Spy Watch™, summoning the Dino-soarer.

"Say what you like about modern spying, Dad, but you have to admit there are times when a hi-tech supersonic jet comes in handy," said Spynosaur.

"The problem with technology is that one comes to rely on it," replied Abner. "What happens when it breaks down?"

"Da-ad, the Dino-soarer's the most cutting-edge flying machine in the world," sighed Spynosaur as they heard the familiar hum of the almost-invisible jet descending. "I hardly think it's suddenly going to..."

Spynosaur trailed off. With his uncanny spy-sight, he could just make out a particularly purple missile streaking towards the Dino-soarer.

"Diaboli—"

The Dino-soarer exploded! Amber didn't even have time to cover her ears before her dad grabbed her. Spynosaur and Abner leaped for cover as flaming wreckage rained down upon the street. They huddled behind fish stalls until the last of the landing wheels bounced along the ground.

Abner got to his feet.
He dusted himself off and
glared at Spynosaur.
"You were saying?"

11.
DA
BIG CITY

Following the loss of the Dino-soarer, the trio of spies were forced to make their way to the big city via a commercial airline. The flight was altogether slower than Spynosaur would have liked – and there was absolutely no tail-room whatsoever. By the time they arrived in the Big City, everyone was aching and exhausted.

"You all right, Dad?" Amber asked with a yawn

as she, Spynosaur and Abner made their way through the airport.

"*Diabolical,*" was Spynosaur's confusing reply. It was the fifteenth time Spynosaur had said "diabolical" in as many hours and he'd said little else for the whole flight. He adjusted his stuck-on moustache and reversible tracksuit disguise as they made their way through passport control. "What escapes me is how the Purple Spyder managed to bring down a spy-jet he couldn't even see! That would take spy-skills as inordinately impressive as, well, *mine...*"

"Nurse your bruised ego on your own time, boy – the only thing that matters now is finding the P.L.O.T. Device," Abner said.

"But without the supersonic speed of the Dino-soarer, won't the Purple Spyder have beaten us here?" asked Amber.

"An excellent point, Agent Amber," Abner said.

"No doubt he will already be under the protection of the mobster, Bronzeface. We must *infiltrate* Bronzeface's criminal organization."

"Or," Spynosaur began, "we could rush in all guns blazing and blow the place to smither—"

"I can't risk losing the P.L.O.T. Device to your ham-fisted swaggering!" Abner sternly interrupted. "We'll use the *spy-chological* approach. We will earn the trust of this Bronzeface. We will persuade him we're his friends. We will convince him to give us the Purple Spyder. Now is the time for mind games."

"Like Pictionary?" Amber asked.

"Sounds like a lot of talking," grumbled Spynosaur. "Do I at least get to wear another disguise?"

Two hours later Spynosaur, Amber and Abner had made their way downtown to Bronzeface's villainous lair. They stood outside the entrance to an unassuming Italian restaurant with a bronze-tinged wooden door. Upon it was a plaque, which read:

WELCOME TO THE VILLAINOUS LAIR OF
DONNIE BRONZEFACE
(Formerly Giovanni's Pizza)

Amber looked up at her dad. In addition to his trusty moustache, he had replaced his tracksuit with an eye-searingly bright pink suit and matching wide-brimmed hat.

"Why don't I get a disguise?" Amber whispered.

"A spy of your calibre does not need a fancy-dress costume, Agent Amber," explained her grandfather, who resolutely refused to wear anything other than his brown suit.

"It's not a fancy— Never mind," Spynosaur said with a roll of his eyes. He kneeled down and put his clawed hands on Amber's shoulders. "The point is, Amber, you're not going to be seen at all — you're going to be invisible thanks to your *sly-spy* stealth suit. I need you to stay out of sight."

"Hmph," said Amber with a shrug. "I suppose being invisible *is* almost as good as a disguise..."

"Finally the boy has sensible advice," said Abner.

For a moment, Spynosaur wondered if his dad was paying him a compliment but then Abner added, "True spies favour the shadows, rather than the spotlight."

Amber activated the top-secret button on her stealth suit. In an instant, she all but disappeared in front of their eyes.

"Ready, Dad?" Spynosaur asked his father.

"Since before you were born," Abner replied. Then he knocked loudly on the door with his cane.

12.
BRONZEFACE

KNOCK.
KNOCK.
KNOCK!

A few tense moments after Abner Gambit knocked on the door it swung open. At first it looked like there was a wall in front of them ... then they realized the wall was a man — a mountain of a man, even taller than Spynosaur and as wide as a small car. He glowered at Spynosaur, his beady eyes barely visible beneath his huge, simian brow.

"Whaddayawant?" the man-mountain said, in a

voice that was so high and shrill that Amber had to clap her hand over her mouth to stop herself from giggling.

"Da name's Jimmy the Tooth ... an' that's the tooth, da whole tooth an' nothin' but the tooth!" said Spynosaur, his accent so thick that Amber could barely understand him. "Dis here is my colleague an' compatriot, Dad Dadson. Me and Mr Dadson got business with yer boss, and it ain't none of yer business what dat business is, so mind yer own business an' let us get down to business!"

"Whadidyasay?" squeaked the confused man-mountain.

Spynosaur was already bored with the conversation. He clenched his fist to strike...

"For goodness' sake," hissed Abner. He jabbed a finger in the man-mountain's barrel chest. "You will take us to Bronzeface this instant or I shall telephone your mother and inform her that, despite your promise to her, you do *not* make an honest living at Precious Paws Home for Neglected Kittens; you are in fact bodyguard to Donnie Bronzeface, Da Big City's most notorious criminal."

"Howdoyouknowaboutmymom?" squeaked the man-mountain, a look of dread on his face. "Don'tsaynothingtoher! Pleasedon'tsaynothing! I'lltakeyoutotheboss!"

Spynosaur unclenched his fist as the panicked giant led them inside the restaurant.

"That was amazing, Granddad!" Amber whispered as she followed invisibly behind. "How did you know all that?"

"Spy-chology, Agent Amber," Abner replied with a smile. "Now to get the measure of Bronze—"

"FIRED! You're fired!" came a cry.

In a shadowy corner of the room, sitting around a large table, were half a dozen men dressed in pin-striped suits and hats. They looked up from their game of Tiddlywinks. The roundest of the men rose to his feet and pointed a stubby finger at the man-mountain. "What did I say about being disturbed on Tiddlywinks night? I said, don't do it, it's my favourite night of the week, best night ever. Squeaks, you're fired!"

"Buttheysaidthey'dtellmymomonmeboss!" the man-mountain Squeaks replied meekly.

"Your mom is a loser," said the figure. As he stepped into the light, Amber could see that his skin had a metallic bronze hue, as did the shock of hair upon his head. "But not as big a loser as you. You're the biggest loser and I'm the biggest winner, everybody says so. I'm very, very rich by the way. I have so much money. Now kick yourself out of here. I want to see actual kicking."

"Yesbosssorryboss," said Squeaks. With a sniff, he made his way out of the door while repeatedly kicking himself in the bottom.

"Forgive the intrusion, Mr Bronzeface," said Abner as Squeaks vanished into the night. "We are most keen to locate an acquaintance of yours by the name of the Purple Spyder."

"Purple Spyder? Great guy, great friend of mine," said Bronzeface. "He did me a lot of favours back when I was starting out. In return I offered him protection, because I'm rich.

I'm probably the richest person ever. I *own* Da Big City ... I own the police ... I own the people. I could go outside and shoot somebody and no one could do anything! OK, maybe not that, but everything except that. But apart from that, there's nothing you can offer me. I have everything I want, twice."

"Oh, I'm quite sure there is something we can give you that no one else can," said Abner.

"What's that?" asked Bronzeface.

Abner was about to answer, when—

"Tiddlywinks!" said Spynosaur suddenly.

"*What?*" hissed Abner angrily.

"Tiddlywinks," Spynosaur said again. "Here's da deal, Bronzeface. I challenge you to a game of Tiddlywinks. If I win, you hand over da Purple Spyder."

"And if I win?" said Bronzeface, "Which I will, I always win, I'm the biggest winner..."

Spynosaur drew his pistol out of its holster and handed it to Bronzeface.

"You can shoot me," he said. Amber clasped her hand over her mouth again, this time to stifle a gasp. Abner slapped his forehead with frustration.

"Looks like we have a deal," said Bronzeface, weighing up the gun. "I make a lot of deals. I'm the best at deals, everybody says so..."

13.

DEATH BY TIDDLYWINKS (AKA DEADLYWINKS)

WEDNESDAY 20:31

BRONZEFACE'S VILLAINOUS LAIR, PART WAY THROUGH A DISTINCTLY TENSE GAME OF TIDDLYWINKS

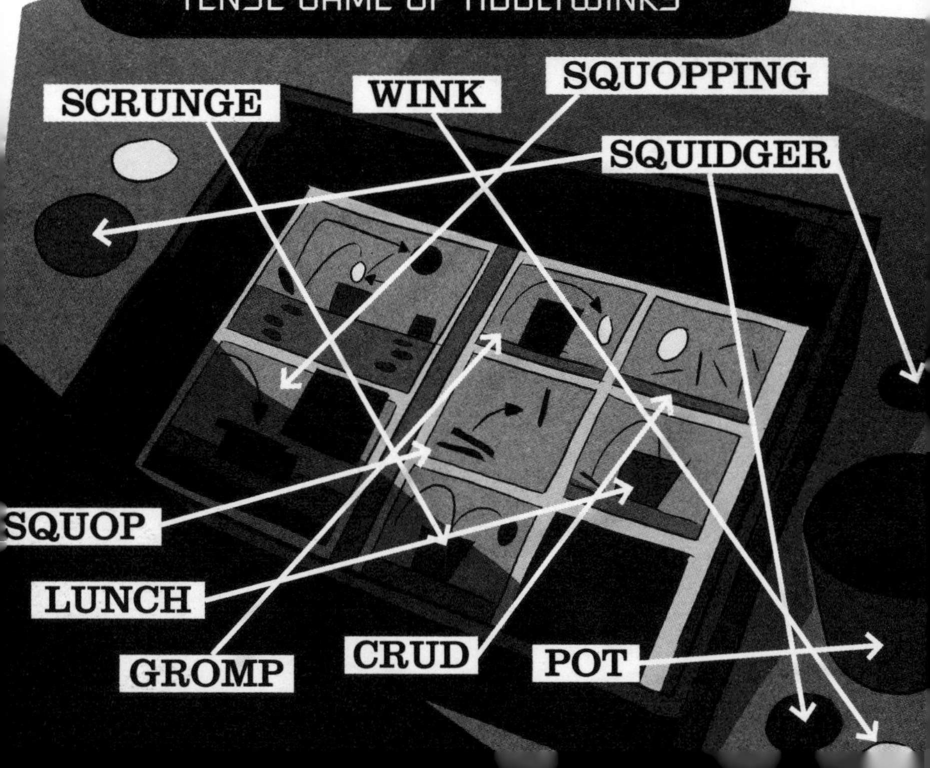

SCRUNGE

WINK

SQUOPPING

SQUIDGER

SQUOP

LUNCH

GROMP

CRUD

POT

The game of Tiddlywinks had been going on for almost an hour, with the disguised Spynosaur locked in a mortal game of who-can-flick-the-most-tiny-plastic-counters-into-a-cup with Donnie Bronzeface. Bronzeface's gathered gangsters looked on, while Abner and the almost-invisible Amber grew increasingly tense with every passing moment.

"Would you please hurry up?" Abner whispered to Spynosaur. "In case you've forgotten, the future of you-know-what is in peril!"

"I think I've added a death-defying *je ne sais quoi* to an otherwise uneventful evening," Spynosaur replied, coolly flicking yet another disc into the pot. "Anyway, it won't be long now – I'm two moves away from victory ... which means we're two moves away from Bronzeface giving us the Purple Spyder."

"You can't win ... I always win ... I'm always the winner," grunted Bronzeface. He hunched over the table, sweat pouring down his face as his trembling hand flicked another disc. With a soft **PONK!** the disc flew off the table and on to the floor.

"Make that *one* move away from victory," Spynosaur noted with a grin. The invisible Amber leaned over the table to get a closer look. It was nearly over.

"Wait! I, uh ... I need a drink!" said Bronzeface, pushing himself up from the table. He stumbled towards a large cabinet at the end of the room and opened it to reveal hundreds of cans of fizzy pop. "Do you want a drink? Have a drink!" Bronzeface said, opening a can. "Everyone says I have the best drinks..."

"Don't mind if I do," replied Spynosaur. Amber didn't need her spy senses to tell her something was up. As Bronzeface busied himself by the cabinet, she crept over to see what he was doing. She watched as he took a pair of tweezers from his pocket, opened a secret drawer in the cabinet, and plucked out a tiny, distressed gerbil.

A Portuguese Poison Gerbil! Amber thought, remembering her spy training...

Portuguese Poison Gerbil

Definitely deadly.
Obviously avoid.
Prevent poisoning if possible.

"Dad...!" Amber said in an imperceptible whisper. As Bronzeface squeezed poison from the gerbil's sweat glands into Spynosaur's can of pop, she raced back to the table, silent and unseen – and gave her dad a sharp kick.

"Ow!" Spynosaur said. The gathered gangsters looked up. "That is to say, 'Ow are you all doing today?" he added.

Amber kicked him again.

"Aah!" he cried. "I mean, ah, Tiddlywinks! The game of kings..."

Another kick.

"Yow!" Spynosaur yelped. "As in, *yow* have all made us feel terribly welcome..."

"You're not seriously going to accept a drink from this man?" hissed Abner, gesturing to Bronzeface. "He is clearly up to something!"

Spynosaur stared his dad in the eyes and said, "Good. I haven't taken an unnecessary risk in hours."

He smoothed his fake moustache as Bronzeface placed a lurid green can of pop on the table in front of him. It frothed and fizzed as if it was about to explode.

"Don't you dare!" Abner whispered.

"*Dad...!*" Amber mouthed.

"Drink!" Bronzeface commanded, desperate to sway the victory. "My drinks are the best drinks!"

Spynosaur picked up the can, ignoring Amber's invisible kicks. Then he turned back to his dad.

"Bottoms up!" he said. And with that, he drained the can of pop in a single gulp.

14.
POISONED

"How ... refreshing," said Spynosaur, wiping his mouth and placing the empty can on the table. "Shall we return ... to ... the ... gaaayyyuuumm?"

"Is something wrong?" asked Bronzeface. "Is something bad happening? Something very, very bad?"

"Jusshht a liddull woooozeeeee..." Spynosaur said as he lost all control of his tongue. Within moments it had swelled up to three times its usual size.

"He can't carry on, I win the game!" Bronzeface

declared as Spynosaur turned a distinctly yellow shade of green. "I win, because I always win, because I'm a winner!"

"Noooo, I caaaan keeeeup playyyyeeeenn…" Spynosaur groaned, his right arm and left leg suddenly going limp. He leaned awkwardly over the table, trying to pick up one of the plastic discs. "I fiiiyuuuuuunn…"

But Spynosaur wasn't fine. Because then this happened:

"You're going to lose, which means I win, which means I shoot you, which means I'm the winner!" Bronzeface said, wafting Spynosaur's pistol in his face – a face so swollen that Spynosaur could barely see.

"Onnne moooore wiiiiiiiink..." he moaned, helplessly. He tried to pick up a wink but now even his left arm had all the strength of the world's laziest newborn baby.

Can't let Dad lose Deadlywinks! Amber thought.

As Bronzeface took aim she leaped into invisible action. Grabbing her dad's hand, she pressed his clawed finger down against the disc. Everyone watched the wink fly across the table as if in slow motion, until...

PONK!

The wink landed squarely in the pot.

"No!" Bronzeface cried.

"Seeeeee...?" Spynosaur groaned. Then he fell off his chair and crashed to the ground with a **FLOMP**.

15.
THE CABINET

"Dad!" Amber whispered as she crouched invisibly over the unconscious Spynosaur. Her grandfather, meanwhile, had other things on his mind.

"We won!" Abner Gambit cried, staring at the Tiddlywinks table. He brandished his cane at Bronzeface, as the mobster's compatriots drew their guns. "You lose, Bronzeface! Now tell us where you're hiding the Purple Spyder!"

"No, no, no! You didn't win! I always win! I'm the winner!" Bronzeface howled. He hurried over to the drinks cabinet and threw his arms around it.

"Wait, that *cabinet*..." Abner muttered.

"You can't have him! I win, not you!" Bronzeface cried, hugging the cabinet tightly.

Abner Gambit's eyes grew wide.

"He's inside," he said. "The Spyder's hiding inside the cabinet!"

The sound of splintering mahogany filled the air and Bronzeface was sent flying (along with several dozen cans of pop) as the Purple Spyder burst out from his hiding place inside the cabinet. The masked menace launched himself on to the Tiddlywinks table and crouched upon it, ready to strike.

"I'll get him!" Amber cried, deactivating her stealth suit. As she reappeared, she leaped at the Spyder with a cry of "**EXCITABLE ELEVENTH ELEGANT ELEPHANT ATTACK!**"

Amber didn't even see the Spyder's counter-attack coming — he swatted her like a fly, sending her skittering across the floor and into a chair.

Abner Gambit sprang into action. As swift as a hummingbird, he darted left and right, swinging his cane in every direction, disarming and dispatching one gangster after another. A scant few seconds had passed before, with **WHACK!** after **THWACK!**, he sent the mobsters crashing through the front door and out into the street. Only Bronzeface remained.

"Protect me, Spyder! Protect me and I'll protect you!" Bronzeface howled in terror. "I have the most money! I have the most tremendous everything! Everybody ... says..."

Bronzeface trailed off as a dark shadow fell over him. He turned slowly to see a looming Spynosaur, more or less restored to a familiar shape. The saurian spy grasped his fake moustache between two clawed fingers and peeled it off.

"S-Spynosaur! The secret agent dinosaur!" Bronzeface bleated.

Spynosaur snarled, showing a mouthful of sharp teeth.

"Get," Spynosaur began as he cracked his knuckles, "OUT."

16.
SPYNOSAUR
VS SPYDER

By the time Amber had dragged herself to her feet, Bronzeface had fled the lair through the shattered door. Only the Purple Spyder remained, crouched upon the Tiddlywinks table.

"Dad, you're OK!" Amber cried.

"Naturally," Spynosaur replied with a wide grin. "I've spent years inoculating myself against the one hundred and fourteen most common poisons. Just a sprinkle of each in my morning coffee stops even the deadliest dose from finishing me off.

Plus, it keeps me regular!"

"It's over, Spyder," growled Abner, rounding on the Purple Spyder. "Give me the P.L.O.T. Device!"

Three generations of the Gambit family closed in on the enemy agent. The Spyder glanced around for a way out ... then looked down at the table.

"He's going for the winks! Get down!" Spynosaur boomed.

The Spyder began mercilessly pinging the plastic discs at his assailants. Winks flew across the room with dazzling speed, embedding in walls and smashing windows. Abner jumped in front of his granddaughter, using his cane to deflect the fast-flying discs, while Spynosaur grabbed one of the cans of pop from the floor. He leaped into action, spinning in the air as deadly winks whizzed past him, before hooking a claw around the can's ring-pull and aiming it at the Spyder's face.

TSSSSSSS!

The jet of pop blasted into the Spyder's eyes, temporarily blinding him. Spynosaur spiralled in the air again, slamming his tail hard upon the table and sending the Purple Spyder flying across the room. He crashed with a **KRUMP!** into a wall and slumped to the floor.

"*Soda* you think he saw that coming?" said Spynosaur with a grin.

Amber forgave the pun; she was speechless with admiration. After such a stylish display, could there be any doubt that Spynosaur was the world's greatest secret agent?

"If you've quite finished..." Abner snarled.

Spynosaur plucked the Spyder's hat from his head. He retrieved the P.L.O.T. Device from inside and handed it to his father. Abner peered at the black cube, his mouth agape.

"At last..." he whispered.

"I'd say that's Mission: Accomplished, wouldn't you?" said Spynosaur, picking up his pistol from the floor and holstering it. "Don't bother thanking me, it's all in a day's work..."

"Thanking you?" snapped a furious Abner. "You needlessly risked your life and the future of spying itself – *twice* – on a game of Tiddlywinks and a fatal fizzy drink! What were you thinking, boy? *Were* you thinking? Or is all this just to try and impress me?"

Spynosaur stared at his dad as he waved the P.L.O.T. Device in his face.

"Dad, I don't think I've *ever* known how to impress—"

SHUNK!

A grappling claw hooked the P.L.O.T. Device and dragged it out of Abner's hand. There was barely time to turn before the claw retracted across the length of the restaurant and placed the device into the hands of the prostrate Purple Spyder.

"Don't be a fool, Spyder!" Abner howled. "There's nowhere to run!"

The Spyder winced in pain as he tried to stand. He glanced at the door but it was too far to reach. He shrugged ... and pressed a hidden button on the wall.

A trap door flew open beneath him, swallowing him into the floor below before slamming shut in a flash.

"OK, he *really* likes trap doors," Amber noted.

Spynosaur narrowed his eyes as a loud, metallic groan filled the air. "But what's he got in store for us?" he asked.

KRUN-N-NG!

As if on cue, reinforced steel walls sprang up from the ground, turning the restaurant into a prison. Which was bad enough ... but then the walls started closing in.

17.
THE P.L.O.T. THICKENS
(AKA THE SPY FLATTENS)

"Another one of Spyder's traps!" snarled Abner, as the room rapidly reduced in size. "He must have rigged Bronzeface's lair decades ago!"

"Talk about a *pressing* concern," said Spynosaur.

Spynosaur, Abner and Amber wasted no time in throwing themselves at the moving walls, pushing with all their might at the hidden hydraulics that threatened to squash them.

"REPELLING ROTOR CHEESE

FONDUE KITCHEN SINK KICK!"

Amber howled, kicking the walls with all her might. She fell backwards and Spynosaur picked her up and lifted her on to his shoulders.

"Did you not think to check the Spyder was unconscious, boy?" said Abner, trying to lodge his cane under the moving wall.

"Like I said, I've never known how to – **HNNF!** – impress you, Dad," replied Spynosaur, shoulder-barging the wall with all his dino-might. "It's always been your way or—"

"My way *is* the way! I was saving the world while you were still a glimmer in your mother's eye," Abner snapped. "It's no mystery from whom you inherited your recklessness! At least she didn't live to see the 'person' you turned into..."

"My mother...?" Spynosaur muttered, pausing from his assault on the wall. He retrieved the silver locket from his pocket and stared at it once more. From her dad's shoulders, Amber squinted to peek at the photograph inside. It was of a lean-faced, honey-skinned young woman she had never seen before. She had long black hair and an enigmatic glint in her eye.

"Dad, is that—?" Amber began.

"And what example are you setting for your daughter?" Abner interrupted as the walls edged ever closer. "What about her future? Do you really want her to end up like *you*?"

"I know you don't approve of my spectacularly impressive methods, Dad," Spynosaur replied. "But for what it's worth, I always tried my best to—"

"Well, your best is not good enough!" Abner cried.

"What's that supposed to mean?" asked Spynosaur.

"Uh, could we maybe talk about this when we're not about to get completely *squished*?" Amber suggested, by now able to touch all sides of the encroaching steel.

"I mean, I have *seen* the secret information held within the P.L.O.T. Device," replied Spynosaur's dad, ignoring Amber's plea. "Thirty years ago, before the Department 6 spy-entists locked the device away ... I peeked. I learned the identity of every spy on Earth. I know everyone born to be spies."

"...And?" said Spynosaur. By now he and his father were all but pressed together.

"You were just a young agent-in-training but I was sure the P.L.O.T. Device would identify you as a spy," Abner said as Spynosaur's barrel chest pressed against him. "But when I looked, your name was nowhere to be found."

"Wait, *what*?" shrieked Amber from her dad's shoulders.

"I'm sorry, boy," Abner added. "But you are *not* a born spy."

There was an inconveniently long pause as the news sank in. Finally Spynosaur let out a saurian snarl and said:

"Then we're wasting our time trying to recover the P.L.O.T. Device ... it's clearly *broken*."

"The device is working perfectly," insisted Abner, his nose now pressed against Spynosaur's. "It correctly deduced the identity of every agent I have ever met and many more besides. The fact is, you don't have what it takes to be a spy."

"I have so many mixed feelings right now but I can't help noticing something," Amber said. "WE'RE ABOUT TO GET SMOOSHED!"

"Excellent point, Agent Amber," said Abner. "Any ideas, boy? Do you have an escape plan or are you going to rely on the spy-entists to bring you back from the grave again?"

Spynosaur grimaced.

"I ... thought ... as much," wheezed Abner. Then with his last lungful of air he spoke a single word:

"*Crumpets.*"

With a sudden **VMMM** and **KRUNG!** the walls retreated and disappeared back into the floor.

"'Crumpets'? Granddad, what's 'crumpets'?" Amber repeated, leaping down from her dad's shoulders. "Wait, was that a top-secret super-spy code word to stop the walls? How did you know the top-secret super-spy wall-stopping code word?"

"It's really very simple," Spynosaur began. "You see, your granddad – well, uh ... that is, he..." he trailed off, and Amber saw a strange look in his eye. It was a look she had seen perhaps three times in her life. Her dad was completely stumped.

"Secrets and spies," said Abner with a wink.

"We don't have time for this now!" Spynosaur growled impatiently. "We have a P.L.O.T. Device to retrieve and a spy to catch!"

With a swipe of his great tail, Spynosaur smashed the trap door to splinters and leaped into the hole.

18.
THE SKY'S THE LIMIT

A CAR PARK BENEATH
BRONZEFACE'S VILLAINOUS LAIR

Spynosaur emerged inside a large, subterranean car park. For once, the Purple Spyder wasn't hard to follow — his sprained left leg had dragged along the ground, leaving a trail of scuff marks. Spynosaur raced after him. By the time Amber and her granddad had followed Spynosaur through the shattered trap door, he was halfway across the car park.

"Dad? Dad!" Amber cried. A moment later she heard the roar of an engine and saw a bright purple car streak round the corner. It wasn't until Abner flung her out of the car's path that Amber realized her dad was clinging to its roof.

"Back in a bit!" Spynosaur blurted as the car sped past. It crashed through the barriers and out into the street. Even in the dead of night, Da Big City was bright with neon and thronged with traffic.

"Time to do something breathtakingly impressive ... I mean, on top of the breathtakingly impressive stuff I'm doing right now," Spynosaur said to himself, digging his claws into the car's roof as it swerved between traffic. "That'll show Dad who's— AAH!"

In an instant, wings shot out from under the car and propeller blades unfolded from between its headlights. Before Spynosaur could even think of a pun, the sky-car took to the air, rocketing upwards, spinning and spiralling past gleaming glass-walled buildings.

"Aerobatic acrobatics won't shake my resolve, Spyder – or my grip!" shouted Spynosaur as the sky-car soared clear of Da Big City's skyscrapers. "I once held on to a sumo wrestler in a paddling pool filled with olive oil for a full twenty-four hou— Uh?"

It took Spynosaur a moment to realize that the Purple Spyder had ejected the sky-car's roof, turning the airborne automobile into a stylish convertible – while simultaneously sending him plummeting to the ground.

"Diabolicaaaaaal!" Spynosaur noted as he fell. He dislodged himself from the roof and – as the ground fast approached – reached for a button on his belt. "This calls for a secret inflatable jet pack!"

With a **SSSSS-CHUNG!** Spynosaur's bright red and chrome jet pack inflated on his back. A **FOOM!** later, the pumped-up propulsion pack propelled Spynosaur through the sky. Within moments he had the Purple Spyder's sky-car back in his sights.

The chase was on.

THE P.L.O.T. DEVICE PREDICTS JUST
WHO IS BORN TO BE A SPY

(IF SPYNOSAUR IS NOT,
THEN SHOULD HE BE ALLOWED TO FLY?)

Hats
off to you,
Spyder!

SPYNOSAUR!

Having swiped the Purple Spyder's hat from his head (and the P.L.O.T. Device nestled underneath it), Spynosaur swooped away. He watched as the Spyder's out of control sky-car careered downwards, crashing on the roof of a nearby skyscraper and skidding to the building's edge.

Spynosaur looped the loop in the air, drawing a picture of his own grinning face in the sky with the smoke trail from his jet-pack. Then he landed on the roof of the skyscraper next to the wreckage of the Spyder's sky-car.

"Now *that's* Mission: Accomplished," he said, reaching into the Spyder's hat and plucking out the P.L.O.T. Device. He examined the jet-black cube with a victorious raise of his eyebrow ... then glanced over at the sky-car.

The driver's seat was empty.

And the Spyder was gone.

19

TOPPEST TOP SECRET

DEPARTMENT 6 HEADQUARTERS,
LONDON

With the P.L.O.T. Device in their possession, M11 agreed to send a Department 6 jet to pick up Spynosaur, Abner and Amber. Despite reeling from the news that her dad was not a born spy, Amber's tiredness quickly got the better of her. She was asleep before the jet arrived and didn't stir until they were back in London. She awoke curled up under a desk and covered with a blanket. After a loud yawn, she spotted her dad's clawed feet. She crawled out from under the desk to find Spynosaur huddled over a computer, tapping furiously at the keyboard.

"You OK, Dad?" she asked, peering over his shoulder. Spynosaur didn't even look up from the screen. "Where's Granddad?"

"He said he was taking the P.L.O.T. Device back to the Department Vault ... where it belongs," Spynosaur replied, his long tail swishing uneasily.

"So why didn't you take me home?" Amber asked with another yawn. "You always take me home after Mission: Accomplished."

"True, but something about all this feels unfinished — and I don't just mean the Purple Spyder's impressive escape," Spynosaur said, typing away. "Something's not right ... I just can't quite put my claw on it."

Amber rubbed the back of her neck.

"Do you maybe think what's bothering you is — is what Granddad said?" she asked, finally. "I mean, about you not being a born spy?"

"Well, it would explain a lot," was her dad's oddly matter-of-fact reply. "Maybe that's why he was always so hard on me ... maybe he knew I didn't have it in me to be a secret agent."

"But that's a hundred per cent nutty spread, isn't it? You're the best!" Amber said, all but stamping her foot. "You stopped the Spyder! You got the P.L.O.T. Device! You drank poison and won at Deadlywinks!"

Amber's dad finally looked up from the computer.

"Actually, it was *you* who invisibly guided my wink to victory — thank you for that," he said with a smile. He gave Amber a hug ... and then returned to his typing. Amber glanced at the computer screen.

INCORRECT PASSWORD.
TOPPEST TOP SECRET ACCESS DENIED.

> INCORRECT PASSWORD.
> TOPPEST TOP SECRET ACCESS DENIED.

> INCORRECT PASSWORD.
> TOPPEST TOP SECRET ACCESS DENIED.

"Why don't you just *ask* Granddad for the toppest top secret password?" Amber suggested.

Her dad tutted and shook his head. "And give him the satisfaction? No chance," he huffed.

Amber sighed, and wondered why grown-ups had to complicate simple things.

"I'm hungry," she said, her belly rumbling. "What's for breakfast?"

"'Breakfast'? Of *course*," Spynosaur declared. He slowly tapped at the keyboard.

> C-R-U-M-P-E-T-S_

"Granddad's top-secret super-spy code word?" said Amber. Spynosaur hit ENTER.

PASSED PASSWORD ACCEPTED.
TOPPEST TOP SECRET ACCESS GRANTED.

"Yes! Clever girl, Amber!" Spynosaur cried as the P.L.O.T. Device appeared on screen. To its left was a file icon marked "D-SPY".

"D-Spy?" said Amber.

Spynosaur opened the file. Another graphic appeared – this time of a domed shape, not unlike an igloo, but constructed from metal, with numerous antennae sprouting from its surface in every direction.

"What is that?" asked Amber.

Spynosaur's eyes grew wide. "Of course ... it's so obvious! This was the plan all along!" he said, leaping out of his chair. "I have to stop him!"

"Stop him? Stop who?" Amber asked.

"Your granddad!" Spynosaur snarled. "I have to stop your granddad!"

20.
AN INCONVENIENT INTERVENTION

Amber pursued her father as he sped through the corridors of Department 6 Headquarters. She had no idea what was going on. Why would they need to *stop* Granddad?

"Spynosaur! There you are!" came a cry, as M11 appeared from round a corner. She blocked their path, looking even more red-faced and flustered than normal. "I-I've been wanting to talk to you."

"Sorry, M11, can't stop, I have to—" Spynosaur began.

"Now hold on, agent. I – *we* – would like to

speak to you," M11 continued in unnervingly soft tones as Dr Newfangle and Danger Monkey appeared behind them in the corridor.

"'Ello, Spyno," Danger Monkey said. "Look, all yer best pals are 'ere..."

"Indeed! We want you to know that we're not just your colleagues, we're your friends ... and we're here for you," Newfangle added.

"Uhhh, what's going on?" Amber muttered.

"I've no idea," Spynosaur insisted as his colleagues advanced slowly towards him. "Now look, the fate of the world depends on me yet again, so I really must be—"

"Abner – Agent A1 – informed us of his discovery," M11 explained, her moustache twitching with despair. "He saw the secret information on the P.L.O.T. Device. You are *not* a born spy."

"Oh *that*," groaned Spynosaur. "Look, whatever you've been told, my dad is—"

"Abner says you ain't got what it takes to be a spy!" blurted Danger Monkey, all but tearing his hair out. "Normally I'd bite someone's earlobes for besmirching the good name of my scaliest friend but we're talkin' Abner Gambit 'ere! When the world's greatest secret agent says someone ain't a born spy, you 'ave to listen!"

"Could we put a pin in this conversation?" Spynosaur snapped. "The important thing is finding my dad before—"

"Denial is inevitable, Spynosaur," M11 said, taking Spynosaur by the hand. "I didn't want to accept the truth either, not after everything you've done for the Department. But Dr Newfangle here assures me the P.L.O.T. Device is one hundred *and one* per cent spy-entifically accurate."

"Well, yes, but—" Newfangle began sheepishly.

"Don't lose your nerve, Doctor – we all agreed we would sit Spynosaur down and talk through his ... problem," M11 insisted, eyeballing Spynosaur. "We're here to help you, Spynosaur. We understand that it's hard to accept you're not a born spy..."

"Fine! I admit it! I'm not a born spy!" Spynosaur growled impatiently. "Now would you *please* get out of my way!"

"Admitting you have a problem is the first step to accepting you have a problem," said an unmoving M11. "And accepting you admit you have a problem is the first step to admitting you accept that you admit—"

SHOOOF!

Spynosaur launched his wrist-mounted spy-net. It spiralled through the air, engulfing M11, Dr Newfangle and Danger Monkey.

"Oi! Lemme out!" Danger Monkey shrieked. "We ain't finished tellin' you that you ain't up to the job!"

"Blast it to smithereens, Spynosaur, release us this instant!" howled M11. "That's an order!"

"Dad, what—?" blurted a baffled Amber.

"I'll explain everything later," Spynosaur said. "Now if you'll excuse me, I have a feeling things are going to start blowing up around here."

21.
ABNER ESCAPES

"Wait, I thought Granddad took the P.L.O.T. Device to the vault," said Amber as she followed a speeding Spynosaur past their captive colleagues and down another corridor. "Isn't the vault in the other direction?"

"Your granddad never went to the vault!" Spynosaur replied.

Rounding a corner, the pair emerged in the Department's vast, underground hangar. Half a dozen sleek jet aircraft were lined up in the cavernous grey space, each one only slightly less impressive than Spynosaur's now-blown-to-smithereens Dino-soarer. In the middle of the hangar was a runway leading to a secret launch tunnel.

"Dad!" Spynosaur boomed.

Abner Gambit was clambering into the cockpit of the nearest jet. He spun round. The first thing Amber noticed was the P.L.O.T. Device gripped tightly in his hand.

"Granddad?" Amber muttered. "What...?"

"Well done, Agent Amber! You caught me red-handed!" her granddad cried. "What a clever secret agent you are. Unfortunately I really must be going..."

"Hand over the P.L.O.T. Device, Dad!" Spynosaur growled. "Don't do this!"

"You'll thank me in the end, boy!" Abner replied, pocketing the P.L.O.T. Device as he clambered into the cockpit. "Now, though I despise theatrics, I really do need to cover my escape..."

With that he activated the jet's retro-rockets, and it burst into life. The jet lifted off the ground, hovering in the air as it pivoted towards the other jets. A moment later, Abner unleashed a volley of missiles, blowing one of the jets to smithereens.

As flaming jet wreckage showered the hangar, Abner fired again – and again – and again, blowing up jet after jet until only his remained.

"DAD!" Spynosaur roared as he saw his father blast through the launch tunnel. Within moments he was gone.

"Well, that was nuttier than a squirrel's lunch," Amber noted, trying to keep her cool. "What's going—"

"Spynosaur!"

M11 strode into the hangar, free of the spy-net and fuming, with Danger Monkey and Dr Newfangle hot on her heels.

"Blast it to smithereens, Spynosaur!" M11 wailed. "This is the last straw! What on earth is—"

"M11, I know you think I'm not up to the job, and I know how much you enjoy shouting at me," Spynosaur said. "But trust me when I tell you that the future of Department 6 ... the future of the free world ... the future of *spying* itself is in imminent danger! My father has just left with the P.L.O.T. Device and I need to go after him ... I need to go back to the North Pole."

"The North Pole *again*?" Amber protested. "But I just thawed out!"

"Very well, agent, I give you permission to go after Ab— Agent A1," agreed M11 with a dubious scowl. "Though since all our jets are blown to smithereens, I'm not sure how..."

"I have just the thing!" Dr Newfangle cried. With the push of a button, a secret wall slid aside in the hangar to reveal an equally secret hangar-within-a-hangar. Sparkling disco lights filled the space, illuminating an enormous, jet-black flying machine. It looked almost identical to the Dino-soarer – but very slightly bigger and a whole lot glossier.

"Presenting the *Dino-soarer mark two*!" Dr Newfangle proudly declared. "Now with added spy-entific splendiferousness! I've been working on it for months – I was going to have it ready for your birthday, Spynosaur."

"Dr Newfangle, you're a marvel," said Spynosaur, racing up the new Dino-soarer's ramp with Amber hot on his heels.

"Wait, I haven't told you about all the new features! Enhanced almost-invisibility ... front and rear science rays ... pine-fresh smell..."

"Sounds marvellous, Doctor," Spynosaur said impatiently. "I promise I'll read the manual just as soon as—"

"Reversible rockets ... convertible rockets ... submersible rockets..." Newfangle continued. "Artificial intelligence ... superficial stupidity..."

"Great," Spynosaur said, "but we really have to—"

"Self-cleaning engine ... self-cleaning thruster .... self-cleaning toilet..." Newfangle carried on. "AAC* ... ATM** ... AAB*** ..."

FWOOOOOSH!

Dr Newfangle's cloud of hair blew across his face as Spynosaur and Amber blasted through the launch tunnel aboard the Dino-soarer MKII.

Newfangle droned on obliviously.

"FAQ**** ... IMHO***** ... LOL****** ..."

*Anti-Aircraft Cannon **Anti-Tank Missile ***Anti-Auntie Blaster
****Fast-Acting Quantumizer *****Idiotic Mandrill Healing Orb
******Lost Otter Locator

22.
RETURN TO THE NORTH POLE

◯ THE NORTH POLE (AGAIN)

The new, improved Dino-soarer MKII raced to the Arctic Circle in a matter of hours. Amber spent the entire journey plaguing her dad with questions about their mystifying mission.

"Why are we going back to the North Pole?"

"Why did Granddad blow everything up?"

"What's a D-Spy?"

"What's going on?!"

"Secrets and spies," Spynosaur replied, bafflingly.

Amber knew there were secrets about her

granddad her dad wasn't telling her. Maybe he didn't know either. Or maybe he was just holding back for dramatic effect.

Either way, by the time they landed at the North Pole, the sky was clear and blue. It was eerily quiet as they disembarked from the Dino-soarer MKII and strode towards Abner Gambit's igloo once again.

"If we run into any more mecha-penguins, remember the plan," said Spynosaur. "Oh, and if you happen to spy something that looks rather like a metal pin cushion as big as a house, be a good girl and let me know."

As if on cue, the ground began to rumble. Within moments, a vast, curved structure rose out of the ice beneath the igloo, lifting it thirty metres into the air. The structure was the same strange dome Amber had seen on the computer screen back at Department 6 Headquarters but with the igloo perched on top of it like a hat.

"Uh, I spy a metal pin cushion as big as a house," Amber said, her mouth agape as she gazed up at the metallic monolith. High above them, her granddad appeared in the igloo's tunnel doorway.

"Amber, I knew you'd find me! Well done!" he bellowed happily. Then he added with a tut: "You took your time, boy ... did you get lost?"

A doorway in the vast pin-cushion structure slid aside at ground level and Amber saw the mecha-penguins waiting to greet them. They gestured Amber and her dad inside with a wave of their wings.

"Well, come on in then, boy," Abner cried from above. "You're letting the cold air in!"

Spynosaur grunted and trudged through the snow towards the entrance, with Amber hot on his heels.

The inside of the metallic pin cushion was cavernous, silver, and a pleasant twenty degrees Celsius. Hi-tech machinery lined the curved walls — massive generators that hummed with power, and whirring, clanking computers as big as filing cabinets. A dozen metal wires thicker than Spynosaur's arm stretched out from the walls towards a huge, transparent sphere in the room's centre, feeding it with so much mysterious power that it glowed.

"What is all this?" Amber asked, her head aching slightly from confusion.

"Your granddad built a giant secret weapon hidden beneath an igloo in the North Pole ... and he accuses *me* of being flash," Spynosaur snarled, glowering at Abner. "I should have seen it sooner – this isn't the Purple Spyder's secret base, is it, Dad? It's *yours*."

"Wait, *what*?" Amber blurted.

"Work that out all by yourself, did you, boy?" said Abner, descending via a motorized platform, which came to rest next to the sphere. He strode towards them, CLACK-ing his cane on the metal floor.

"But what's it all for, Granddad?" asked Amber,

peering at the sphere as it pulsed with power.

Abner shrugged. "You know how it is – secrets and spies…" he replied, patting one of the mecha-penguins on the head.

"No, Dad – no more 'secrets and spies!'" Spynosaur growled. "No more lies or mind games or spy-chology! Amber deserves to know the truth … and she deserves to hear it from her grandfather. Tell her what you've done … tell her about Project D-Spy."

"So you've seen the Toppest Top Secret files? I'm surprised you managed to decipher them." Abner glanced at Amber, who stared back in nervous confusion. He threw his arms up. "Oh, very well! It's too late to stop it now, anyway. My dear Agent Amber, I present to you *Project D-Spy*! Please, look closely at the sphere…"

The huge, central sphere glowed so brightly it was hard to look at but after a moment Amber realized there was a dark shape suspended in the orb's centre – a jet-black cube.

"That's the P.L.O.T. Device!" Amber cried. "What's it doing floating around in there?"

"An excellent question as ever, Agent Amber. You see, that wondrous cube is just *part* of this masterpiece of engineering known as the *D-Spy Machine*," her granddad replied. "The P.L.O.T. Device is the machine's *brain*, so to speak. And now machine and brain have been reunited, I can finally put Project D-Spy into action."

"But what *is* Project D-Spy?" Amber asked in frustration.

"A solution! No, a cure! No, a— Oh, I'll leave it to them to explain," said Abner.

The robo-penguins moved closer, their heads ratcheted back in readiness.

But instead of attacking, they sang a surprisingly tuneful song.

23. ABNER'S GAMBIT

AND NOW WITH THIS REFRAIN WE SHALL EXPLAIN!
REVEAL THE SECRETS!

YOUR GRANDDAD HAS A PLAN THAT IS QUITE GRAND
IN ITS UNIQUENESS.

HE WON'T MAKE ANY FRIENDS!
HE WILL NOT MAKE AN A-POL-OGY,

HE'LL USE HIS MIGHTY MIND,
AND SPY-CHOL-OGY!

REGRETS! FIDDLE-DEE-DEE!
IT'S PLAIN TO SEE THAT HE'S NOT LYING,

HE'LL WIN WITH THIS MACHINE, FULFIL A DREAM

GET RID OF SPYING!

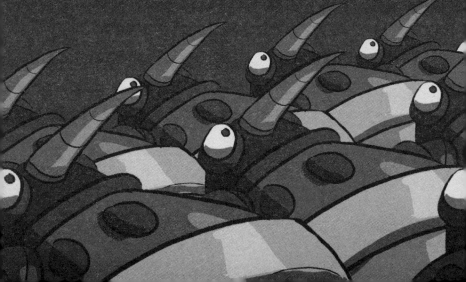

HE'S BEEN A SPY SO LONG, DONE RIGHT AND WRONG,
RODE LOW AND HIGHWAY,
HE'S SPENT A BITTER LIFE, STUCK IN THE SPY WAY!

YES, IT IS TRUE, HE'S HAD ENOUGH!
OF SPYING AND SPIES, IT'S NOT A BLUFF

WORK IT OUT - IT ISN'T TOUGH!
JUST LOOK AROUND AT ALL THIS STUFF!

NO MORE SPIES! WHAT A SURPRISE!
THAT'S THE **DE-SPYYYY** WAY!

"There! The truth is out!" Abner said, as the penguins' mechanical jaws clamped shut. "Project D-Spy is really Project *De*-Spy! Do you see, Amber?"

"Uh, no," Amber replied with a shrug. "And that penguin song was super confusing."

"Your granddad plans to de-spy every secret agent on Earth," Spynosaur explained, glaring at his dad. "He wants to make spies like everyone else ... he wants to make us *normal*."

"Wait, *what*?" Amber gasped.

"I didn't expect you to agree with my plan, boy – you've got too much of your mother in you," Abner sneered. "But I cannot tell a lie..."

Spynosaur snorted derisively.

Abner turned to his granddaughter. "The truth, Amber, is this," he continued. "Some forty years ago, one week after the birth of your father, I ordered the Department 6 spy-entists to design a machine capable of identifying and *de-spying* every secret agent in the world. It would send a pulse of pure de-spying energy across the globe, powerful enough to reduce even the most super super-spy to an average, common-or-garden human being."

"Diabolical," Spynosaur snarled.

"The spy-entists had their doubts, too, boy," Abner continued. "So once the plans were complete I set about building the machine myself, away from the prying eyes of Department 6. It took years of secret visits to this base to complete..."

"Is *that* why you used to leave me with Grandma Gambit all the time?" Spynosaur growled. "*Doubly diabolical.*"

"But little did I know, the Other Side had discovered my plan," Abner continued. "They sent the Purple Spyder to stop me. As the countdown began, the Spyder stole the P.L.O.T. Device, rendering the De-Spying machine useless.

I intercepted him as he tried to flee the igloo and we fought. The Spyder's freeze-bomb went off, and for thirty long years my plan was—"

"Put on *ice*," Spynosaur interrupted. He gritted his teeth. "But now that *I've* rescued the P.L.O.T. Device from the Purple Spyder, you're back in business."

"What do you want, a medal?" snapped Abner. "Believe me, I offer something much more valuable – no more spies!"

"But why, Granddad?" Amber asked, a funny feeling in her stomach.

"That's the one thing I haven't been able to work out either," said Spynosaur. "*Why?*"

"Because I *hate* spying!" Abner cried. "There, I said it! I hate spying and everything about it!"

"Now look, Dad, you can say what you like about me," Spynosaur growled, "but I won't have you bad-mouth spying in front of my daughter!"

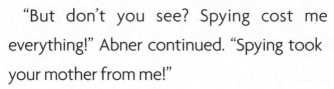

"But don't you see? Spying cost me everything!" Abner continued. "Spying took your mother from me!"

"My mother? What about my mother?" Spynosaur said.

Abner exhaled. "She was a spy, boy," he said at last. "Your mother ... was the world's greatest secret agent."

24.
MUMS AND MECHA-PENGUINS

"My mother ... was a spy?" Spynosaur muttered.

"The best of the best," explained Abner. "But she, too, worked for the Other Side. I met her on a mission. We were meant to kill each other, if I recall. Instead, it was love at first sight."

"Eww," Amber muttered. "Love and spying don't mix..."

"What happened?" asked Spynosaur grimly.

"*You* happened," Abner replied. "After our mission ended, your mother and I went our separate ways. I heard nothing from her — but I could think of nothing else. Then, nine months later, she appeared out of the blue with *you* in tow. I was delighted! I thought it was a chance for your mother and I to leave our lives of spying behind and start a *new* life together as a family! But your mother's only loyalty was to spying – everything else just got in the way. That included me ... and you."

Spynosaur clenched his fists. Amber heard his knuckles crack.

"Dad...?" she muttered. "Are you all right?"

"She left me ... left me with nothing but this," Spynosaur said, taking the silver locket out of his spy-suit. "She left us both, didn't she, Dad?"

"I never saw your mother again. From that moment, I *hated* spying," Abner said. "You, on the other hand, grew to share your mother's maverick ways – though not her natural-born spy skills."

"So you insist on reminding me..." Spynosaur replied.

"But today I reset the clock! A clean slate —
a chance for us all to start again!" Abner cried.
He climbed a set of steps up to a metal gantry,
atop which sat the de-spying machine's control
podium. The machine's computer screen read:

>> POWER AT 96% <<
>> 3 MINUTES TO DE-SPYING <<

"It may be three decades late, but in three *minutes*
I de-spy the world!" Abner cried with glee.

"Shut this machine down, Dad! It was Mum
who betrayed us, not spies! Without spies the
world will fall into chaos!" Spynosaur said, fists
clenched. "I'll stop you if I have to..."

"Stop me? Arrogant pup!" Abner scoffed. "Do
you think I'm not prepared for more interventions?
Have you forgotten I have *mecha-penguin power*

on my side?"

The man-made musical mecha-penguins' heads ratcheted back once again, and they waddled threateningly towards Spynosaur and Amber, preparing to unleash a sonic assault.

"Amber, now!" Spynosaur ordered. In a blur, he and his sidekick leaped into action.

"HUNDRED BUNNY FLYING SLIPPERS HOT CROSS BUN ATTACK!" Amber cried as she and Spynosaur spun in the air, their flying kicks sweeping the mecha-penguins' legs out from under them and sending them crashing on to their backs. They lay on the ground, flapping and wheezing helplessly.

"Sorry, Dad, your penguins seem to be lying down on the job," said Spynosaur.

"Oh, I didn't mean them," Abner began coolly. "I meant *him*."

A secret door slid aside at the far end of the base.

The first thing Spynosaur and Amber heard was the thunderous **BOM-BOM** of approaching flipper-steps. Then they saw it – a penguin, twenty metres high.

"Behold, the *mega* mecha-penguin! And he's not going to sing to you, boy – he's going to give you a jolly good hiding," said Abner.

Spynosaur and Amber looked on as the massive mega mecha-penguin waddled towards them.

>> POWER AT 97% <<
>> 2 MINUTES TO DE-SPYING <<

"What do we do, Dad?" asked Amber as the colossal robo-bird loomed over them.

"Just another day at the office, Amber," said her dad, striking a battle-ready pose. "It's time to punch a giant robot penguin in the face."

Without warning, the mega mecha-penguin's head exploded! As shards of molten metal showered to the ground, Spynosaur looked up.

Atop the glowing sphere of the de-spying machine, wielding an impressive purple bazooka, stood the Purple Spyder.

26.
REVERSE SPY-CHOLOGY

"Dad!" Amber cried, scrambling to her feet as the mega mecha-penguin toppled to the ground. "It's the Purple Spyder!"

"Another *colourful* entrance," said Spynosaur. He watched the Spyder leap down from the de-spying machine, landing both feet squarely on Abner's chest. The Spyder and Abner flew from the platform and bounced along the ground like skittles. Neither remained there for long. In moments both were back on their feet and squaring up to each other ... but Abner was a split-second faster. He struck the Spyder on the jaw with his cane, knocking the hat from his head. The Spyder crumpled, unconscious, to the floor.

"Dad, stop!" Spynosaur cried. As he and Amber raced towards Abner, all three of them spotted Spynosaur's pistol on the floor, knocked from his scaly grasp during the battle with the mega-mecha-penguin.

"I won't be thwarted again! Stay out of this, all of you!" Abner howled.

"*Spy* don't think so!" Spynosaur cried, once again launching his wrist-mounted spy-net. It flew towards Abner but he ducked, sliding on his knees under the airborne snare and plucking the pistol from the floor with the tip of his cane. He flipped the gun into his hand and pointed it at Spynosaur.

"Stop!" he cried. "I mean it, boy. Don't think I won't do what I have to!"

"Then do it!" Spynosaur roared, skidding to a halt. "Shoot!"

"What? Wait!" Amber howled, leaping between her dad and granddad. "Family doesn't shoot family!"

"Amber, you're too young to understand but I promise you it will be better soon," Abner said. "Once everyone is de-spied, *everything* will be better!"

"That would sound a lot less nutty if you weren't pointing a gun at my dad," Amber said. "And also ... **FLASH FRY HIDDEN MITTEN SCOTCH EGG BLAZING AMAZING ATTACK!**"

Spynosaur barely had time to shout, "Amber, wait! Stop! Don't do it! No! Wait! Stop!" before his daughter was flying through the air, her feet aimed at delivering a decisive ninja kick right in her granddad's face ... but with another deft duck, Abner scooped his granddaughter's leg with his cane and sent her flying across the room. She collided with one of the de-spying machine's generators and was knocked out in an instant.

"Amber!" Spynosaur roared. He turned to his father, shaking with rage, his snarl exposing a mouthful of sharp teeth. "Dad, that's *enough*. You've gone too far."

"And what are you going to do about it? In case you've forgotten, you're not even a born spy!" Abner said, pointing Spynosaur's gun at his chest. "I'm sorry, boy, but I can't let you stop me!"

>> POWER AT 99% <<
>> 30 SECONDS TO DE-SPYING <<

"Let ... you ... stop— Of *course*!" Spynosaur cried, slapping a clawed hand on his forehead. "Finally it all makes sense!"

"What makes sense?" asked his father. "What are you talking about?"

"All those years of spy training ... every time you told me I wasn't good enough, you knew it would only make me work harder to become the world's greatest secret agent," Spynosaur cried. "Even yesterday, when you told me I wasn't a born spy, you knew it would just make me test my limits. You wanted me to stop you! You were using reverse spy-chology on me!"

"*Reverse* spy-chology? What poppycock!" Abner cried, the gun suddenly shaking in his hand. "Why – why would I want to be stopped?"

"Because, deep down, you know you're wrong, Dad," Spynosaur replied. "You began my training at the exact same time you came up with your plan to de-spy the world. Whether you knew it or not, you were training me to be your conscience. You made sure I was a cut above the rest – even you! You trained me to defeat you!"

"I-I won't hear this! I won't!" Abner screamed. Perhaps it was because his hand was trembling as his finger hovered over the pistol's trigger ... perhaps not. Either way, a moment later, Abner Gambit fired.

Abner slumped to the ground.

"Turns out I'm an *uppercut* above the rest as well," said Spynosaur, blowing on his fist.

>> POWER AT 100% <<
>> DE-SPYING COMMENCING <<
>> DE-SPYING COMMENCING <<
>> DE-SPYING COMMENCING <<

"No!" Spynosaur cried as the de-spying machine pulsed with raw de-spying energy. Within moments it would engulf the Earth. Spynosaur grabbed his pistol from the floor and aimed it at the de-spying machine, when:

"*Ahem*," said a voice.

Spynosaur spun round. Behind him was the Purple Spyder, his purple bazooka resting upon his shoulder. Spynosaur ducked as the bazooka's missile streaked over his head with a

SHOOOOOOF! – and headed straight towards the de-spying machine.

In a flash of bright white light the de-spying machine exploded, showering the base in a fiery cascade of metal shards. Spynosaur grabbed his dad and leaped towards Amber, covering them both with his massive frame as flaming wreckage rained down.

By the time the smoke had cleared, Spynosaur was charred and blackened, but in a better mood than he'd been all day. Amber and his father were still unconscious but unhurt – Spynosaur had taken the brunt of the blast. He stood up and dusted himself off.

"You – ow – certainly have a knack for blowing stuff to smithereens, Spyder," said Spynosaur. He turned to see the Purple Spyder drag himself to his feet and shake the debris from his purple coat. "My dad never approved of that sort of thing," Spynosaur added. "I always wondered where I got it from ... but now I know, don't I?"

Spynosaur took the locket out of his pocket and threw it to the Spyder.

"It's good to finally meet you," he added. "*Mum.*"

The Purple Spyder opened the locket and stared at the photograph inside. After a moment he reached up and pulled off his spider-emblazoned mask.

"Hello ... son," the Spyder replied. Beneath the mask was the woman in the photograph –

lean-faced and honey-skinned, with long black hair and an enigmatic look in her eye. "It's been a long time," she continued in a warm voice. "Although you appear to have changed a lot more than me. I've been dying to ask, why are you a dinosaur?"

"It's a long story," Spynosaur replied.

"Well, since we saved the future of spying – and most likely the world – we have a little time on our hands," said Spynosaur's mum, returning his locket. Then she reached into a pocket in her coat and took out a packet of purple crumpets. "Fancy a catch-up?"

20.
FAMILY TIME

Amber awoke to the smell of purple crumpets toasting. It's fair to say she was gobsmacked to discover the Purple Spyder was her grandmother. But Abner, as it turned out, had known all along.

"I was trying to spare your feelings, boy," Abner explained, rubbing his swollen jaw. The family had gathered round a makeshift fire made from chunks of still-smouldering de-spying machine as they toasted their crumpets. "I thought if you knew your mother was alive and trying to stop me, it might ... raise questions," Abner added. "And make you less inclined to help me retrieve the P.L.O.T. Device."

"And I suppose *I* was hoping to avoid a family reunion," confessed Spynosaur's mum. She handed Spynosaur a crumpet. "I wasn't sure how you'd take my abandoning you as a baby, and since I'd been doing the whole silent-spy routine for so long, it seemed easier just to keep it up."

"So, wait," said Amber, rubbing her temples. "You knew who Granny was the whole time, Granddad? And Granny, you knew that Granddad knew?"

"And *I* knew, too – eventually," said Spynosaur with a wink. He took a bite of purple crumpet and smiled a toothy smile. "'Crumpets' ... that was your *failsafe word*, wasn't it? In case you got each other into a scrape you couldn't get out of. *That's* how you stopped the walls closing in, back in Bronzeface's lair."

"Well, just because your parents want different things, it doesn't necessarily mean we don't love each other — or that we want each other dead," said the Purple Spyder.

"These last two days have been nuttier than a nut factory," said Amber, chomping down a crumpet in three quick bites.

"That's families for you," said Spynosaur. He turned to his father, still nursing the bruise on his chin. "So, what now, Dad? I'm pretty sure I can't face the prospect of locking up my own father like a criminal. If I let you go, do you absolutely promise not to try to de-spy the world again?"

"Honestly? No," Abner confessed. "It has rather become my mission in life."

"I thought as much," Spynosaur said with a roll of his lizard eyes. "Well, at least you know if you concoct any more mad schemes, I'll be here to stop you."

"Don't try and take all the credit, boy," huffed Spynosaur's dad. He picked a bit of de-spying machine debris from his hair. "Yes, I may have lied about you not being a born spy, but if I hadn't you might never have found it in yourself to defeat me. Or to put it another way, you're welcome."

"How is that— Never mind," Spynosaur sighed.

He turned to the Purple Spyder. "And, Mum, I don't suppose you fancy becoming an agent for Department 6?"

"I'm afraid not – this is about as much 'family time' as I can take," the Spyder replied. "Plus, I can't stand children. No offence, Amber."

"No, that's fine," said Amber sarcastically. "Totally an OK thing to say to your own granddaughter..."

"Still, as I have missed all of your birthdays while frozen in a block of ice, you're probably overdue a present," added Amber's granny. She produced her purple bazooka from behind her back and handed it to Amber. "Here you go. One missile left – use it on whatever you like."

"Really?" Amber squealed. She took the bazooka in both hands and the weight of it almost toppled her over.

"Wait, what about missing all of *my* birth— Never mind," sighed Spynosaur.

29.
KEEPING WARM WITH THE HELP OF A BAZOOKA

An hour later Spynosaur and Amber stood in the snow outside Abner's secret base, watching Abner Gambit and the Purple Spyder go their separate ways. Abner jetted into the air in the Dino-soarer MKII (after promising to tell Spynosaur where he left it) and the Purple Spyder sped through the snow on a purple sled drawn by purple huskies.

"Are you sure it's a good idea to let them go?" Amber asked, propping up her new purple bazooka. "Especially as we now have no way of getting home…"

"I'm sure M11 will send someone to pick us up eventually," Spynosaur said, transmitting their coordinates to HQ via his Super Secret Spy Watch™. "Anyway, I thought it might be nice for the *two* of us to have some family time."

"Definitely," said Amber, hugging her dad tightly. After a good, long squeeze, she said into her dad's ear, "I knew Granddad was telling porkies ... I knew you were a born spy."

"Amber, take it from someone who was turned into a dinosaur, it doesn't matter how you were born," Spynosaur said. "I'm a spy because I *choose* to be a spy ... and because I'm clearly the best at it by a mile."

"Double definitely!" Amber chuckled, staring out into the snow. "But I'm even gladder that you're my dad."

"So am I," he said, rubbing his daughter's arms as she shivered. "Are you cold?"

"Well, it *is* the North Pole," Amber replied, breath puffing out of her mouth.

"What say we warm things up then?" Spynosaur suggested, pointing to Amber's bazooka. "One missile left – care to do the honours?"

"Really?" Amber said excitedly. She lifted the bazooka on to her shoulder. "But wait, what if it's ages till we get picked up? We're a million miles from home and this is our only shelter. Should we really blow everything to smithereens?"

"Some things we choose," said her dad. "And some things run in the family."

Amber grinned and pointed the bazooka in the direction of Abner's secret base. She paused.

"Dad, how *did* you know the Purple Spyder was your mum?"

Spynosaur smiled.

"It's very simple," he said. "We first met the Purple Spyder on a Thursday. Thursday was originally called 'Thor's Day'. Thor is the God of Thunder. Thunder follows lightning. Lightning strikes the Earth every second. Second is the first loser. The most commonly lost household item is..."

As her dad went on, Amber decided she didn't really need to know. So she took aim at the base, and:

HE'S THE SPY THAT SURPRISES!

HE'S THE AGENT WHO'LL AMAZE!

FIGHTING FOR RIGHT, THANKS TO THOSE

SUPER-SCIENCE RAYS

HIS DAD NEEDED DEFEATING

'CAUSE HE'D REALLY LOST THE PLOT

SO SPYNO WON THE DAY

- AND DIDN'T FIRE A SINGLE SHOT!

SPYNOSAUR!

SO IF YOU NEED A HERO WHO'S A CUT ABOVE THE REST

THEN DO WHAT ABNER GAMBIT DID

AND PUT HIM TO THE TEST

AMBER AND HER FATHER ARE ON HAND TO SAVE THE DAY

AND BLOW STUFF UP TO SMITHEREENS
IF IT GETS IN THEIR WAY!

SPYNOSAUR!

SPYNOSAUUUUUR!

CLASSIFILES

CODE NAME:
SPYNOSAUR

AKA:
Agent Gambit, A47

Primary Spy-ciality:
Advanced Spying

Secondary Spy-ciality:
Puns

Motto:
"I'm going to make
crime extinct."

With the brainwaves
of top super-spy Agent
Gambit and the body
of a Deinonychus,
Spynosaur is the
world's only Super
Secret Agent Dinosaur!
Specializes in
stylishly saving the
world, defying death
and infuriating his
boss, M11. Spynosaur is
an expert combatant, a
cunning detective and a
master of disguise ...
as long as no one spots
his tail.

DEPARTMENT
6

CODE NAME:
AMBER

AKA: Amber Gambit,
"Dad's Little Poppet"

Primary Spy-ciality:
Ninja stuff

Secondary Spy-ciality:
Spy stuff

Motto:

"SURPRISING NAIL
CLIPPERS TWISTING
TERRAPIN ATTACK!"

Spynosaur's daughter
and sidekick, Amber
Gambit is as dedicated
as her dad to fighting
crime and foiling
fiends wherever they
find them. Highly
resourceful and
skilled, with more
ninja moves than you
can shake a foot at,
Amber Gambit keeps her
double life and ninja
skills secret - even
from her mum.

DEPARTMENT
6

MISSING IN ACTION

CODE NAME:
AGENT A1

AKA:
Abner Gambit

Primary Spy-ciality:
Spy-chology

Secondary Spy-ciality:
Spy-ence

Motto:
"To understand how your
enemy thinks, think like
your enemy."

Once considered the
Department's greatest
secret agent, A1
wrote the rulebook on
spying, as well as
an advertising jingle
for Whitewash Fabric
Detergent. A1's greatest
weapon is his mind,
which is as sharp as
the sword hidden in his
cane. Vanished while
on a mission that was
so top secret even he
didn't know what it was.

DEPARTMENT
6

MISSING, PRESUMED PURPLE
<<UPDATED>>

CODE NAME:
PURPLE SPYDER

AKA:
The Mauve Menace,
Purply McSpyface

Primary Spy-ciality:
Mysteriousness

Secondary Spy-ciality:
Purpleness

Motto:
"..."

An agent of the Other
Side, an international
spy agency once in
competition with
Department 6 for secret-
keeping. The Purple
Spyder was their most
prominently inconspicuous
secret agent. Also,
it turns out she's
Spynosaur's mum. Who'd
have guessed? Did you?